RATS

PAUL ZINDEL

HYPERION PAPERBACKS
NEW YORK

First Hyperion Paperback edition, 2000

1 3 5 7 9 10 8 6 4 2

Printed in the United States of America.

LIBRARY OF CONGRESS CATALOGING-IN-PUBLICATION DATA

Rats/Paul Zindel—1st. ed.

p. cm.

Summary: When mutant rats threaten to take over Staten Island, which has become a huge landfill, fourteen-year-old Sarah and her younger brother Mike try to figure out how to stop them.

ISBN: 0-7868-0339-8 (trade)

ISBN: 0-7868-2820-X (lib. ed.)

ISBN: 0-7868-1225-7 (pbk.)

[1. Rats—Fiction. 2. Staten Island (New York, N.Y.)—Fiction. 3. Science Fiction.] I. Title.

PZ7.Z647Rat 1999

[Fic]—dc21 98-47192

Visit www.hyperionteens.com

CONTENTS

1 • THE FESTERING

His first day back from the Fourth of July vacation, Leroy Sabiesiak knew he'd get some good target practice with the rats in Area 17. "Garbage Siberia," he muttered to himself as he mounted his bulldozer. He checked the stubble on his leathery face, made certain his flask of vodka was tucked into the hip pocket of his overalls, and left the main sanitation depot at 7:05 A.M. He headed the bulldozer out past the asphalt cover of the dump to what was left of the open garbage.

He was glad the dump was nearly sealed. He'd been working there from the beginning, before it had the fancy name of the Staten Island Landfill. Two decades of breathing the reeking garbage was enough. In a few weeks he'd be retired, start collecting on a fat pension with health and dental, and it'd be time to dream.

He kept his eye out for rats as he edged the bulldozer along the south rim of the asphalt. The mall was across the highway. On his right was one of the new black mountains of tar. "I'm gonna miss ya," he yelled at the smothered dump. "Yeah, I'll miss ya."

"Hi, guys," Leroy called out as he drove the bull-dozer onto the freshly dumped garbage and saw the first few rats of the day scurrying across the top of a heap of meat scraps. "I'm gonna see a lot of ya buy the farm today!" he said, stopping to grab his BB gun and fire off a few shots. "It's gonna be my little farewell present to ya all!" Leroy knew he would have gone nuts if he hadn't made a game out of the rats from the beginning. He could hit a rat on the run at fifty feet. Hit it right in the face. About that, he was very proud.

Leroy had noticed the increase in rats over the last few weeks. He'd shot hundreds of them, but there were so many, he'd taken to bringing along city-issued packets of poison that he'd dip in peanut butter. "Ya love peanut butter, don't ya, fellahs?" Leroy shouted at the rats. He knew they loved peanut butter more than anything else. Their next favorites were sardines and beer! "Love yer poison with a little fish and brew, don't ya!" He could always tell when rats had gotten a good dose, because the poison would react with the rats' diges-tive juices and puff them up with gas. The rats would swell up to twice their size before they died a horrible, painful death.

Ehhhh. Ehh.

He'd hear them dying. In their last hour they'd stagger over the top of the dump like drunk balloons. Leroy loved pumping their bloated bodies full of BBs. He'd hit them dead in their eyes, making their eyeballs pop and leak and explode out of their sockets.

Leroy spotted a fresh pile of dumped appliances and furniture. He left the bulldozer motor running and got down with the BB gun to check things out. "Lookin' for a good refrigerator," he mumbled. "Wouldn't mind findin' a decent cuttin' board, either." Half his house was furnished with stuff he'd found at the dump, including a twenty-one-inch mahogany TV picture-in-picture and a SWAP button.

BING. BING.

He got off a few good shots at the bloated rats on top of the body of a dead collie somebody had thrown out with the trash. People had no respect anymore when it came to what was legal garbage and what wasn't. He plodded farther away from the bulldozer and pulled his boots up as he sank deeper into the garbage.

For a while he forgot about the time and enjoyed shooting every rat he could. When he turned to start back to the bulldozer, he noticed a half dozen very large rats sitting on a distant ridge of garbage.

BING. BING.

He fired at them one after the other. He hit several of them right in the head. Dark red fluid gushed out of their mouths and ears. He was about fifty feet from the bulldozer and went after another line of fat rats that appeared on the highest ridge.

"I'll shoot ya in yer ears!" Leroy yelled at them. "In yer ears and yer bellies. I'll hit ya where it hurts!"

He spotted a swollen mother rat trying to salvage her nest of straw and threads and bottle caps. In a moment he was standing over her, pumping her mouth full of lead pellets. He saw her naked, furless babies, barely able to move, and he shot each of them, too. Their heads burst off their bodies, and he laughed.

He was laughing when the first rat bit him.

He hadn't seen it coming. He remembered the line of them on the ridge, but suddenly, one of the rats turned and raced across the top of the garbage. Before Leroy could do anything, the rat was in the air. It landed on his shoulder, digging its claws into his collarbone and sinking its chisel-shaped front teeth into his back.

"Whoa!" Leroy yelled. "What are ya doin'? What do ya think yer doin'?"

Leroy reached around and grabbed the rat by its wet, oily fur. He tore it off of him along with a strip of his own skin, punched the rat, and hurled it away across the dump. For a few moments he tried to laugh, but he was too surprised by the attack. Confused. He couldn't think of anything funny to tell himself. That was when he felt something he'd never felt before.

Something like . . .

Like fear.

It was the sight of a hundred—two hundred!—rats that came over the ridge as a unit. "Ya keep away from me!" he shouted as the rats inched closer. His voice was empty now. Hollow. He felt his arms begin to shake and his belly drew into a chilled, rock-hard knot.

CHIRRRRR. CHIRRR.

The rats made low sounds like some sort of large, half-muted fowl or seabirds. As they advanced, the garbage made its own crackling noises from under the army's weight. His tongue grew thick and dry, and his eyes started to tear and burn. His instincts told him to get out of there.

Fast.

Get back to the bulldozer.

Leroy started off, but his boots sank deeper. He got less than ten feet before he noticed several dozen of the rats had ducked into the garbage and were writhing beneath the debris in front of him. Thick brown bodies, some as large as a foot, slithered like shining fish beneath the surface of a muddy pond. They closed in and climbed swiftly to the surface. A dozen rats began to bite at Leroy's legs as he spun around, swinging the butt of the BB gun.

"Ya get away from me! Ya get away!"

Several larger rodents from the ridge were airborne now. They landed as a single clump on Leroy's neck, biting him deeply. The rats hung on tight, like a living, gnawing scarf as he screamed. Twenty—thirty—rats were biting at his legs now, ripping open veins and arteries as they tripped him.

"Nooooooo!" Leroy cried, trying to crawl the distance to the bulldozer. There was a flurry at his groin, and he doubled over like a fetus as rats with large front teeth began to gnaw through his T-shirt and into the folds of his stomach.

Another mob of rats rushed Leroy, and his body began to convulse. His whole being shook violently, desperately trying to throw off the feeding rats. The wounds of his abdomen were larger now. Bloodier. Gashes two and three inches wide. Several smaller, muscular rats scooted in to wiggle their heads into his wounds. The rats crawled under his skin, their sharp, relentless teeth chewing through his layers of stomach fat toward the moist, curling warmth of his intestines.

Leroy was on his side, his legs flailing, striking out against a rusted ice chest that lay on a ruptured mattress. He could feel the rodents *inside* of him now. Moving. Squirming. At last a wail bubbled up through his frothing lips, a treble scream of pain and shock and amazement.

Air and lymph gushed from Leroy's mouth, and his eyes froze open and suddenly glazed. There was a final reflex, a gentle quivering of his body, while his steaming entrails spilled out like snakes of chalk into the morning air.

2 • SARAH AND MICHAEL

The wind blew the stench from the garbage dump so that it fell in sheets of drenching, putrid waves, coating the cars and house shingles and even the rugs inside homes as far as ten—even twenty—miles away! Sarah Macafee, fifteen, walked along the edge of her lawn with her brother, Michael, ten. My God, I've grown used to the smells and the rats and the huge mountains of garbage, Sarah told herself. *I've gotten used to them.*

"You want to come with me this morning?" Sarah had asked Michael when she was going out with her box of Save-the-Sanctuary chocolate bars. "I want to see if any of the neighbors want to buy any more." The Woodland Bird Sanctuary was Sarah's high school's favorite charity. It had been mainly the pizza and cake sales by the New Springville students and PTA that had saved the wildlife refuge from becoming part of the dump. Thousands of birds—migrating night herons and storks and eagles—all kinds of creatures had been spared from death and from becoming part of the huge black mass that stretched out in front of her.

"Will the asphalt stop the stink?" Michael asked, proudly walking Surfer, his pet white rat. "Will it stop the bad smells?"

"Dad and the other supervisors think it will," Sarah said. She stooped for a moment to straighten the leash on Surfer's tiny harness, then stood up to survey the closest capped mountain of garbage. People hadn't been upset about the dump in the beginning. Travis and New Springville were districts, towns, at the edge of the swamplands, the useless lands on Staten Island. There had been creeks to swim in and kids went fishing and crabbing and muskrat hunting.

Even when she was a child, her father had taken her for walks and they would eat the wild plums and watch the small silvery killies swimming in the tidal pools. She knew her father held on to his dream that covering the dump with asphalt and making it into a city park would bring everything back. Bring back all that was clean and living and green. And bring back good real estate prices, too.

"What's that noise?" Michael asked.

Sarah listened. At first she heard only the screams from the cloud of seagulls above the last of the open tracts. The gulls swooped and ravaged pockets of freshly dumped garbage at the end of the asphalt lid. They took to the air clutching rotting pork ribs and mold-covered bread and tin cans alive with beetles. Soon these last open tracts, too, would be sealed.

"The gulls?" Sarah asked. "Are you talking about the noise of the gulls?"

"No. The noise from *there*." Michael pointed to the edge of the asphalt where one of the garbage dump mountains had been graded to the level of the Macafee lawn.

Then Sarah heard it, too. It was like a buzz, a nearly imperceptible vibration. "That's probably from the jets flying over. They've changed the take-off and landing patterns from the airports; from Newark, JFK, and LaGuardia, and even the old Stewart Air Force base. All the planes fly over us now. All the jumbos. Their roar shakes the earth. Shakes the whole dump. The sound resonates." She realized after the word left her lips that Michael wouldn't know what *resonates* meant. "Bouncy sound," Sarah said. "Like an echo. Yodel-o-eee-ho!" Michael laughed at her explanation.

Sarah loved it when her brother's face lit up with understanding and his mouth broke into a smile. He hardly ever talked or laughed since their mother died. It had been a year. No. A year and a half now—since her death. Sarah blamed the dump for that, too. If it hadn't been for the dump, they would not have haphazardly expanded the roads leading to the mall. There would have been more thought, more planning for stop signs and crosswalks and traffic lights.

There would have been safety islands. A chance for her mother to get across Richmond Avenue with Michael, to make it from the end of Springville Gardens to the mall Burger King and the kids' meals and the silly prizes and the carousel. Mrs. Macafee would have been able to keep Michael by the hand. There would have been time before the drunk kid in the SUV shot out of Travis Road and floored it. Mrs. Macafee had pushed Michael out of harm's way, but the car had struck her with a sickening thud. Witnesses had testified that she had been thrown into the air, tossed like a rag doll. They said they heard the sound of her body hitting the soft metal of the car's hood and the unforgiving glass of the front windshield. . . .

Sarah stopped the memory. She tried not to think about the death of her mother and how much she missed her. How much her father and she and Michael . . .

She held Michael's hand tighter. She told everyone

she had the best brother in the world. He was strikingly good-looking, with long blond hair that sprang magically from black roots. She had always wanted his hair; not the straight clumps of brown strands that descended from her own scalp like lusterless parentheses.

Michael's deep blue eyes were intense with need and curiosity. It wasn't his fault that he was a painfully shy and nervous boy. He was cute. One day everyone would see how grown-up and confident and normal he could be, Sarah always told herself. No matter what the tests or the school psychologist or any of the neighbors on the block said. No matter that his classmates made him do things like put thumbtacks on teachers' chairs or tape crazy notes on girls' backs—no matter how many neighborhood brats picked on him and called him "Stupid Mike!" and "Crybaby Rooster Head!"—Sarah knew her brother was doing the best he could.

All the Macafees were.

Now she heard more clearly the sound from the asphalt-covered dump. CHIRRRRR. CHIRRR. She had heard it before, this sound that made her think of danger. Dread. There was something wrong about the way they had covered the garbage with truckload after truckload of black pitch. The strange sounds had woken her up the very first night after they had covered up the garbage. There had been different sounds in the beginning. Like a moaning coming from the black mounds. She had mentioned the sounds to her father. "Maybe it's the methane expanding," her father had said. They shouldn't have tarred over all the pipes—all the small chimneys that had let the gas escape from the dump, Sarah thought. She didn't know what the sounds were.

"The noises wake me up at night," she had told her father. "There's something wrong. I don't know what the noises are, but they seem louder at night. Strange sounds. The rotting garbage is making methane. It's got to be building up and expanding. The whole dump could become a big bomb."

"You've got quite an imagination," her father said.

"But Dad," she had said. "There's no way for all the gas to get out. The asphalt company didn't leave enough vents. That dump probably needs thousands of vents. There's never been a garbage dump this big in the world. Nobody knows what could happen!"

Her father thought for a moment. "There'll be

cracks. The methane'll leak out somehow," he said, but she wasn't sure he really believed that at all.

"Can we bring Surfer with us?" Michael asked. "He always helps us sell more candy."

"Sure," Sarah told him.

She and Michael started their trek through their sprawling housing development. There was no end to split-level ranch houses lining the east border of the garbage dump. Richmond Estates was the next development to Springville Gardens—and that was all Cape Cod–style homes. The other major housing tract was Holly Farm Homes, the cheapest built of them all, on the south side of the dump. Sarah knew for a fact that the walls of the houses there were paper-thin.

Sarah held tight to Michael's hand as they walked up Wilde Circle. They noticed Miss Lefkovitz sitting in her vintage Toyota, warming up the engine. "Hi, Miss Lefkovitz!" Sarah called across the street to her. Sarah and Michael could see only the silvery wisps at the back of Miss Lefkovitz's French twist. She didn't turn around. "She can't hear us," Sarah told Michael. "She's probably listening to the weather report or one of her oldies-but-goodies on the car radio."

Miss Lefkovitz had bought eight chocolate bars

the day before as a treat for her summer English class at PS 18, so there was no point in bothering her again. She had been Sarah's teacher for two years at the New Springville School, and Sarah loved her. She was the only high school teacher with a doctorate in Chaucerian studies, but she was the daughter of a rabbi and too sensitive for her own good. Whenever she read an excerpt from "The Miller's Tale," boys threw Magic Marker tops and chalk at her.

"We'd better sell the candy bars before it gets too hot," Sarah said, rearranging the chocolates in the box so their wrappers were all faceup and shining.

"Right," Michael said, clutching his pet rat to his chest. "Can we eat one later?"

"Yes, Michael," Sarah said. "Like we always do."

Sarah was proud of the way Michael had gotten over his fear of the rats at the dump. When the family first moved to Springville Gardens, Sarah had been terrified of the rats, too. She had been so scared of rats when she was ten years old that she wouldn't go out of the house. That was when her father had sat down and told her all about rats. He explained how they'd always been around on Earth. How they traveled on ships. And how Sarah didn't have to be afraid of anything furry. Not really. He taught her that it was fun to pet furry things. Cats and ferrets and gerbils.

"But I'm afraid of rats," Sarah had said to him. "Rats give me nightmares, and they're horrible, and I think they want to bite me." She had seen a show on TV about how rats can climb into cribs and bite babies who had milk still on their lips from their bottle.

"Rats don't usually attack humans unless they're cornered," her father had explained. And then he did the best thing he could ever have done. He took Sarah to Pet World at the mall. He let her touch the dogs and guinea pigs and the mice. He let her see how gentle they were. That was when she saw Surfer in a cage and fell in love with him. Surfer was a baby rat then, as white and tiny as a cotton ball. His two glistening pink eyes seemed to be staring at Sarah.

"I want him," Sarah had told her father. "I want the baby white rat."

"Then he's yours," her father said. "But you'll have to take care of him."

"I will, Dad. I promise I will," Sarah said. "He'll be like a cousin to the big brown ones at the dump. He won't ever be lonely. And he can watch TV and play computer games like Creature Feature and take baths with me."

"He's going to get bigger, you know," her father said. "At least six inches and a tail to match."

"Good," Sarah said. "I want him big and strong and brave. Not afraid of anything." They had picked out a habitat cage and exercise wheel and food pellets. Sarah remembered feeling like she was a mother to Surfer. She remembered holding the cute little rat for the first time, nurturing it. Now she was teaching Michael the same way she had learned.

"Surfer is our friend," she always told Michael. "We don't have to be afraid of rats. Not at all."

Mrs. Carson looked out her picture window and saw Sarah and Michael down the block starting to knock on doors. Oh, God, *more* chocolate bars. She didn't want to buy save-the-sanctuary candy. She didn't want Girl Scout cookies or vegetable seeds or vitamins or to order anything from some kid's Christmas catalog. She didn't want to sign any political or environmental petitions. All she wanted was a little peace and quiet so she could finish toilet training her darling son, Kyle.

"You need to use the potty?" Mrs. Carson asked Kyle. Kyle laughed, pulled at his diapers, and continued playing with his stuffed animals in his crib.

She knew from looking at her son's face that he had to go, so she scooped him up, ran with him downstairs, and took off his diaper.

"Use the toilet, honey," she told Kyle.

Kyle laughed again. He watched his mother for a while. He knew there was something about the big white cold bowl that she wanted him to do. "Mama," Kyle said, running to the toilet bowl. He heard something splashing inside of it.

"Mama," Kyle repeated.

"Yes," Mrs. Carson said. "Use the potty."

Kyle looked in the bowl and he saw something moving. Something looked back at him and dived under the water. It disappeared down into the bottom of the toilet.

Kyle started to cry. He ran to his mother, wanting to tell her what was in the bowl. One of those things from the garbage dump, Mama, he wanted to tell her. There's one of those *things* in the toilet bowl.

Mrs. Carson looked up. "Don't be afraid," she told Kyle gently. She looked over to the toilet bowl and realized she had forgotten to clean it for him.

She took a can of cleanser from beneath the sink cabinet and sprinkled a shower of its white powder into the bowl. She knelt down on her knees in front of the bowl and grabbed the gold-plastic handle of the toilet brush and began to thrust its bristles down into the water, prodding and poking at the stains. She was sorry she'd left her reading glasses upstairs. She leaned over the bowl now and scrubbed harder at a stubborn stain.

Suddenly, she was aware of a brown shape beginning to swell up from the bottom of the toilet. At first she thought it was a wet rag in the eddies of the bowl. She had to get it out of the bowl before it completely clogged it. A voice from somewhere in the back of her mind said, *Be careful . . . careful now . . .* but she didn't have time to really listen to it. Whatever it was, she wanted it out now.

A moment later she had pried it loose enough to know it was something furry. A piece of a play fur or clump of lint from the drier. There were always hairy fists of lint collecting on the filters, easily flammable wisps that she had meant to place in a water trap or special sealed bag where a loose spark wouldn't find them. She saw the piece of fur twitch, lifelike. So often she had mistaken pieces of lint for a spider or beetle or moth. She felt a little frightened that it might be something alive, but that didn't make much sense. Whatever it was, it was too big—and it was loosening, starting to come up toward the surface.

By the time it was clear that it was a living thing, it was too late. In a flash, Mrs. Carson's instincts interpreted the movement as beyond the parameters of anything inanimate. Concern, apprehension, and even fright raced electrically through her as the *thing* swam upward in the bowl. She felt her stomach turn and tighten, and a wave of coldness gripped her torso. Blood rushed to her head and her eyes focused sharply, suddenly, as whatever it was broke the surface of the water. Her heart shook as she realized a head with snout and teeth was exploding—erupting!—straight at her.

Mrs. Carson jerked her head back and away, but the large rat had launched itself into the air now. Its body was sleek, with powerful legs and claws digging into the air. Mrs. Carson screamed, and swiftly slammed down the toilet seat. She had a single moment to push Kyle away from the bowl into a pile of laundry and get to her feet.

She ran to pick him up, wanting to get him out

of there, but the seat on the toilet was banged open. Before she could get to Kyle, the powerful and wet writhing body of the huge rat was half out of the toilet and heading for her. She held Kyle as the rat leaped from the bowl and charged at her. With her free hand she grabbed a broken mop and swung it with full force. At first she missed, stroke after stroke, and she settled instead for diverting the dark, snarling mass. It scooted like a shadow, a horrible stalking shadow that closed on her feet. She leaped and stepped to one side faster than she knew, and an innate ability to battle replaced any thought of fleeing. Blood rushed into her head, and her brain pounded as she brought the stick down on top of the rat. Again. And again.

For a few moments the rat kept coming, but then she hit it so hard, it was knocked back toward the toilet bowl. Mrs. Carson was beyond thought. Beyond terror and rage. She began to kick at the huge rat, kick maniacally with Kyle screaming in her arms. She kicked and clubbed at it with the mop handle—wildly!—ferociously!—until somehow the rat managed to crawl back into the bowl. It was in the toilet, diving back down beneath the surface of the water, but Mrs. Carson raced to the toilet and thrust the mop handle after it. She screamed with outrage and fury—matching Kyle's howls—as she thrust it like a sword, hard and deep, and only a long time later, when she realized and believed—truly believed that the rat was gone—only then did she let herself burst into tears.

3 • INVASION

Sarah and Michael were halfway around Wilde Circle when Mrs. Carson ran out of her split-level ranch house carrying her son. "Help," she called, hoarse and dazed. She turned in slow circles, looking across the lawns and driveways and flower beds. She hoped neighbors would hear her and leave their elaborate gas barbecues and laughing guests and wicker gliders. She needed help. Advice. There was only Sarah and Michael on the blazing hot pavement. Sarah realized something was very wrong.

"What's the matter?" Sarah asked. She handed Michael the box of candy to hold and rushed to Mrs. Carson. "There are rats coming up out of the sewer. Out of my toilet," Mrs. Carson managed to utter. Her breathing was shallow. Gasping. "There are rats in my toilet."

Next door to Mrs. Carson's split-level ranch house, the Saturnawitzes' children swam in their backyard pool. The surface was dark blue from the reflection of the sky on the chlorine-sparkling water and black bottom tiles. Jackie Saturnawitz, ten, the oldest boy, sinewy with trim muscles and long thin legs, was the first to notice the curious shadows venting from the side drains of the in-ground pool. At first he thought it was a cluster of magnified oak leaves caught in a backflow from the skimmer, or a shadow-string of geese passing over on the way to the Woodland Sanctuary.

"Time us! Time us!" two of his younger sisters called from the far end of the pool. Before he could stop them, the girls had launched themselves into the air. They landed with big splashes. Sandra Saturnawitz was nine, stronger and older than Jennifer. The two of them raced with Australian crawls, heads submerged and executing wild, earnest strokes followed by a side toss of their heads to grab air, then submerging their heads once more.

Linda, five, the youngest of the Saturnawitz children, watched from her perch straddling a plastic alligator float. She was filled with a strange mixture of envy and joy as she watched Sandra and Jennifer churning the water and racing toward her. She wished she was old and powerful enough to be racing with them. Old enough to go on sleepovers and tall enough to ride Montezuma's Revenge and the Batman roller coaster at Adventure Land.

The waves from the race began to toss her, to

vibrate and shake the alligator, and she braced herself for more thrilling splashes and waves as her sisters neared her end of the pool. Something made her look at Jackie. She saw her brother wasn't timing his sisters like he usually did. He was staring at the water in the far end of the pool, his eyes wide with what looked like surprise or wonder.

"They're racing!" Linda called to Jackie. "Why aren't you timing them? *Why?*"

She watched her brother move quickly along the side of the pool. The splashes of darkness in the water no longer seemed like shadows of birds or floating leaves. A moment more and he recognized the shape of the shadows heading straight into the paths of Sandra and Jennifer. His legs began to weaken and he felt his throat closing with fright. He fought to open his trembling mouth as a cluster of small brown heads broke the surface near Linda on the float.

For a moment longer, Jackie wanted to believe that he was seeing things. He wasn't at the pool at all. He was in a movie house. Or watching a video somewhere. Something he might have seen at the zoo or in the images from a program on India or a South American jungle. His mind had to be short-circuiting. A vision from a terrible dream. But he felt the wind in his face and the coldness of the tile trim beneath his feet. What he was seeing was real.

"RATS!" he began to yell. "RATS IN THE POOL!"

Linda saw them next from her perch on the alligator float. She had heard the words Jackie yelled, and thought it was one of his pranks. He always did things like this. Make fake bats out of crepe paper and set them above a closet door. And the badger in the cage. That was his most frightening trick: their mother's foxtails hanging out of a wooden box with a spring that sprang open and the fox tails came hurtling out—and she screamed and screamed. But she knew in the pit of her gut this was not a joke.

She knew from the terror in his voice, and the sight of the tiny heads with the big teeth heading for her. She shrieked and pulled her feet up out of the water so her entire body was atop the plastic alligator. Sandra, then Jennifer, glimpsed the swimming dark forms ahead as they raced toward them and the end of their water course. They saw them as blurred, wiggling shadows through their swim goggles. Water had seeped into the goggles through the cheap rubber trim, and a mixture of air and chlorinated water played havoc with their sight.

The girls were in the middle of the shadows before they saw the brown oily bodies, glistening clipped fur, and savagely clawing feet clearly. They saw the tiny black eyes burning above flat, wide teeth and wriggling white underbellies. The sisters stopped, frozen in the middle of the school of rodents. They stood still in shock. The girls' limbs strained against the pressure of the water, and dread rippled through their bodies. They tore off their goggles and began to scream. Sandra and Jennifer rushed toward the steps at the shallow corner of the pool, hitting at the rats to clear a path. Their fingers and hands smacked into the slippery bodies and ghastly, snapping faces as more—larger!—rats surfaced around them.

Jackie was afraid for little Linda on the float. Several of the larger, aggressive rats had clawed their way up onto the alligator's plastic tail. Linda's pulse quickened, throbbed crazily, as the first of the rats made it up onto the float. It looked at her and began to scurry along a corrugated seam toward her. It was happening like slow motion, like the sun had become a stroboscope and her eyes could only bear to see half of what was happening. A moment later several more of the gasping creatures had left the water and were shaking themselves on the raft as they advanced.

Linda felt her throat tighten and hurt as though her glands themselves had filled with fear. The rats reached her legs and began to bite at her rubber pool shoes. The creatures were close enough for her to see the pool dribble leaking from their mouths and strands of shiny, thick mucus sliding from their nostrils. Panic began to ride her, shake her to her marrow. The surface of her skin prickled, revolted, as though bathed in a nightmare. A nightmare beyond reason and thought and imagination. The dread of rats had been programmed into her young genes, into centuries of being human. Into mankind's long evolution and deep, deep cry to survive.

One of the rats jumped forward and landed on her shins. With its teeth snapping, it began to run up toward her face. Linda's body trembled in a primordial reflex. She turned and looked dazed, helplessly, to her brother. Jackie had grabbed the long handle of the pool skimming net. She saw him swinging the net out at the plastic alligator and the rat that was on her chest now. The rat sprung again. Linda saw it in the air, its claws reaching for her face. But somehow it was in the net. Her brother had netted it, and hurled the rat like something in lacrosse. He swung the net and pole and knocked several of the other rats off of her and back into the water. But the attack was rough. Too sudden. Linda felt herself losing her balance and falling. She screamed as she went over and splashed down into the pool.

"God! Oh, God," Linda cried as her long, fragile blond hair fanned out in the water. She felt the rats swimming into it, yanking at it, their feet getting caught in it. The tiny claws of a few of the rats reached her scalp, dug in, and tried to crawl up the back of her head. One of the smaller, stronger rats reached her forehead and raced across her brow. It dug its rear claws into her hairline and tried to bite at her eyes.

Jackie threw down the skimming net and dove toward his sister from the side of the pool. Beneath the surface, he saw the twitching, tiny faces and shiny, pronounced front teeth. The wall of bubbles and tiny black eyes and thrashing bodies of the rats blurred into a vision from a bad, bad dream.

Sarah and Mrs. Carson heard the children's screams from the Saturnawitzes' backyard. They ran toward the howling, Michael trailing behind them. They saw Jackie Saturnawitz pulling his little sister from the pool. Wiggling, terrible dark things were dripping from her shiny golden hair, and a thin line of dark scarlet blood flowed down from her forehead. Her sisters stood shivering and screaming on the grass far from the edge of the tossing water.

"Rats! Rats!" they shouted over and over, their jaws shaking and cold with stark fright.

Mr. Ellis heard shouting from the Saturnawitzes' yard. He sat submerged in his bubbling Jacuzzi next door. The Saturnawitz kids were always yelling and shrieking and having pool races and he'd learned to block out their usual racket to enjoy a good long soak. The bubbling of the Jacuzzi was a pleasant sound, a mesmerizing gurgling that cloaked any noisy traffic and the blasting CD player of the Saturnawitz kids.

He liked to slouch in the hot tub with his body immersed all the way up to his mouth. It was soothing and serene to have the hot water and bubbles whip and dance about his chin and ears. He liked to stretch out and let his legs and arms float limply in the agitated water. It was totally relaxing and for a while he closed his eyes.

But he felt something.

Something unusual.

Something that brushed against his legs. At first he thought it was his own bathing suit that had filled with bubbles from the air jets and snapped at his thighs. A moment later, he felt other things. Things gliding past and colliding with his heavy calves and calloused feet.

With his eyes closed he decided it had to be a towel or a T-shirt someone had forgotten. It must have made its way into the Jacuzzi. The noises from the Saturnawitz kids were much louder than usual, he decided. He began to dream of planting trees. There wasn't enough money now. He wanted a new car first, but he'd been told by the Travis nursery that October was the best planting month for trees. A lot of his neighbors had forsythia bushes and rhododendrons. Bushes would be all right to filter street-level noise, but he wanted trees. He'd always loved dogwood, and there was often a good buy on large pines. . . .

The collisions against his legs became more frequent, tickling him and disturbing his soak. Reluctantly, he reached down along his body to try and snatch up whatever it was, but it was elusive. The currents beneath the surface were strong, powerful, and he had to trap a corner of it against his leg and grab for it. *There!* he told himself. He had it now, his hand grasping a thick wad of what felt like a plush towel. He felt its rich, deep terry cloth pile. He opened his eyes to get a look at it as he lifted it up to the surface.

Mr. Ellis watched his hand leave the water. The clump of towel was darker, coarser than what he had expected. It took another moment for him to realize that what he was clutching was not a towel but a squirming, wriggling rat.

He started to scream—a high-pitched scream like that of a woman.

His hand was locked on the rat. Drop it, drop it, he told himself. He fought his way past panic and terror to loosen his fingers, to let the wiggling rodent fall into the water next to him. Now he knew why the children were screaming.

It was no game.

Something had happened to them, too.

A dozen thick, dark rats burst onto the surface next to him. He threw himself away from them and toward the hidden cement steps of the Jacuzzi. He tripped on the first step and his body plunged into the maelstrom of bubbling water. He stumbled, crawled to find footing. Glancing over his shoulder, he saw the rodents swimming for him. He found the first step, began to lift his body from the water. As his face rose above the surface, he saw the Jacuzzi's main drain. There was something strange about the drain. In place of the powder-blue plastic flap that usually swung above the filter basket, there was a type of hairy, greasy brown mound.

"Whaaa . . . ?"

The full word didn't escape his mouth before the mound had a face. A huge rat flew out at him from the drain, its teeth locking on his throat.

Sarah, Mrs. Carson, and the Saturnawitzes' parents heard Mr. Ellis's scream and ran across the lawn to reach him. When they saw him, he was shrieking, trying to lift his overweight body up and out of the slippery, tiled Jacuzzi. The rat dropped loose from his throat, and the powerful jets and bubbles made Mr. Ellis look like he was standing in a huge cauldron. He splashed spastically at the rats that circled him at the surface like squirming, fat leeches.

Another neighbor, an elderly, frail man, who had come outside to adjust his lawn sprinklers, hobbled toward the Jacuzzi to try to help get Mr. Ellis out and to the safety of his patio. The rats surfaced and resurfaced in the gushing water. Sarah thought to throw the power switch off. As the water calmed, the invaders disappeared back down into the drains from which they had come.

"Are you all right?" Sarah asked Mr. Ellis.

"I don't think they bit you very deeply," Mrs.

Carson said, pressing a towel against his throat.

Mr. Ellis took the towel from her, held it himself, and stumbled away from the Jacuzzi. The Saturnawitz children had raced over, afraid to be left alone in their yard. They stood shaking. Linda held her hand over her forehead. The bleeding had stopped.

"What's happening?" Mrs. Carson said, her voice cracking. "Why are the rats doing this? Why are they attacking people?"

Mr. Ellis's oldest daughter, Elizabeth, had run into the cabana tent and brought him a can of anti-septic spray. He took it from her and covered his body with its cold white mist. "Rats carry disease. Fleas. Bubonic plague!" he muttered, his eyes red and watering. Sarah helped him sit in a white plastic lawn chair. A couple of other neighbors had come out of their houses. One of them helped clean the bite on Linda's forehead. Sarah saw Michael frozen on the sidewalk clutching Surfer.

One of the neighbors said, "There were rats at the movies last night. Right in the theater. A lot of people felt them running over their feet in the dark. They screamed, but put their feet up on their seats and kept watching the movie and eating their nacho chips and popcorn and pretzels. Nobody cared. They had paid."

"What are we going to do?" Mrs. Carson fought to hold back tears. "I'm not going back in my house. I have a baby. A little boy. How can I sleep there? How?"

"Call the police and the Department of Health," the Saturnawitz parents said. "We have to call the Environmental Protection Agency! There's something wrong. Very wrong." Mr. Ellis stared at Sarah as though noticing her for the first time. "You're the Macafee girl, aren't you? Your father's in charge of the dump. Does he know what's happening? Does he know about the rats? We'll sue the Sanitation Department. We'll sue him!"

Sarah heard Michael gasp. She knew Mr. Ellis yelling at her about their father frightened him. "It's all right, Michael!" she called to him. She tried to keep her voice steady for his sake, to let him know everything would be okay. "I'll go tell my father now," Sarah said backing away. "I'll call him. He's usually in meetings all day, but they'll put me through."

"I called him this morning and he wasn't in his office," the neighbor said. "I told his snotty assistant, and they haven't done anything about it! Not even the courtesy of calling me back. He's the supervisor of the landfill, isn't he? What is he going to do?"

Sarah scooped up Surfer onto the top of the candy box, and took Michael's hand. "He'll do something." She headed quickly back down the way they'd come.

"We're not waiting for him!" Mr. Saturnawitz called after her. "We're calling the police!"

Sarah felt her heart pounding. She hated it whenever anyone said anything against her father. There were always things happening at the dump. Terrible smells. Flooding. She hated her father's job, a job where everyone complained and was nasty to him. No one ever called about anything good, or said, oh, Mr. Macafee, thank you for taking care of the garbage dump. Thanks for managing the mountains of our waste and junk and debris, and for letting us hurl and throw and fling away everything and anything we want. . . .

"Mr. Ellis didn't mean to be yelling about Daddy," she told Michael.

"Why are the rats coming up into people's drains?" Michael asked. "Why are they biting people?"

Sarah looked off to the huge black asphalt hills that were the dump. "I don't know," she said, but she had warned her father. There would be methane. Methane building underneath. Poisonous gas that could be dangerous.

They were halfway home, passing Miss Lefkovitz's house, when Sarah noticed the teacher was still sitting in her car. There was something about the angle of Miss Lefkovitz's head that was strange, as though she were stretching her neck or straining to see something in front of her.

"Wait here," she told Michael. "I want to tell Miss Lefkovitz about the rats," Sarah said, starting across the street. As she got closer to the car she saw the driver's window was open. There was no sound of a radio. No music or weather report. Sarah had always loved saying hello to Miss Lefkovitz. Miss Lefkovitz's voice was gentle and delicate. She always wore silk dresses and beautiful earth colors and a delicate rose perfume.

"Miss Lefkovitz," Sarah said, walking up the driveway. "Miss Lefkovitz . . ."

Sarah realized something wrong. Miss Lefkovitz didn't turn toward her. Both her arms were at her sides. Sarah reached in toward her, touched her on her shoulder. Suddenly, Miss Lefkovitz's head swung toward her. In place of the wide smile and kind familiar eyes, Sarah stared into a frozen mask. Sarah's hand recoiled, her entire body shuddered, and she muffled a scream. Sarah saw claw marks on the leather of the dashboard and side panels. Miss Lefkovitz's eyes were open, her mouth agape and stiff. Her eyes stared ahead.

Shocked.

Amazed.

Stunned in death.

4 • SHADOWS

Mack Macafee's mind was reeling long before his daughter reached him by phone. Ever since his wife's death he'd been nervous and anxious. It was a deep-seated feeling that the world was no longer a place to trust. The world was not safe for his children or him, or anyone for that matter. He cursed the split-level ranch house he'd bought in Springville Gardens. He'd bought it for a song because of its location smack next to the dump. At the time, the whole family thought it was a great buy, that the landfill would only be used for a few years and then turned into a beautiful park.

He believed that if they hadn't moved there, his wife would still be alive.

All the house had ever brought him was bad luck, and this week had started off with more of the same.

His meeting at the borough president's office had been interrupted all morning long by phone reports of rat bites and rats popping up out of toilets in the tract homes surrounding the dump. And the two top priority events: Miss Lefkovitz and the sanitation worker. The police had already notified the office of Bea Lefkovitz's death.

"At least her body's in one piece," Lt. Vivona had reported. "Not what the sanitation workers found out on the open dump. Not what was left of Leroy Sabiesiak." At noon, when other operators had checked the still-running, abandoned bulldozer, they could barely recognize what was left of the cadaver as being human. Only Leroy's flask and BB gun helped confirm that the mound of raw flesh and half-eaten skull had once been a man.

"I had to call his brother in La Jolla," Mack said. "It was the hardest call I ever had to make in my life. Sabiesiak had nieces and nephews. He kept their camp photos and school drawings up in his locker. They were hoping he'd come out and live with them."

"At least you didn't have to bag the pieces and watch the coroner scribble 'devoured by rats' on his death certificate," Vivona said. "What's going on? *Devoured* by rats!"

"You fix this," the borough president had practically yelled at Mack. "You fix this *fast*."

Mack left the St. George offices with John Medina, his main assistant at the landfill project. Macafee was in his early forties, a gentle giant of a man with his head thrust forward and forehead freckled from too much sun. John was ten years younger than Mack, always wearing a faded Mets baseball cap and a T-shirt, meetings or no meetings.

The dump had been part of Mack's life since the beginning when he'd first gone to work for the city, driving one of the specialized carting trucks used at the landfill. He even remembered back when folks from all around Staten Island drove to the wetlands to throw their garbage out their car windows. The smells then were mainly from the U.S. Steel and American Cyanamid plants. All the big New Jersey factories and refineries across the Arthur Kill Waterway. There were other plants in Linden and Bayonne. That's where the first rats and rankness had come from, not the dump.

As Mack cut through Willowbrook Park and turned left onto Richmond Avenue, the familiar sight of the huge black mounds of the dump came into view.

"Like we didn't have enough problems without rats surfing in people's toilets," John said. "And rats eating people, we definitely didn't need."

"Yeah," Mack said.

He got a sinking feeling inside of him—the feeling that the real nightmare was just beginning.

"When is Daddy coming home?" Michael asked.

"Soon," Sarah said. "He said he'd be home soon." She had made Michael leave her alone on the porch while she watched the police and ambulance workers dealing with Miss Lefkovitz up the street. Sarah didn't want Michael to see her crying. Images of Miss Lefkovitz's face haunted her: Miss Lefkovitz smiling in a classroom, praising her for a story she'd written in English class about a scientist who cloned a dozen Hemingways; Miss Lefkovitz running the annual spelling bee; and Miss Lefkovitz in death.

The coroner's van was a black station wagon with dark-tinted windows. Sarah watched them as they put the teacher's body into a black rubber bag, and slid her into the back of the wagon like a rug. *What are you going to do, Dad?* she thought. *What?*

"I can't find Surfer," Michael called out. Sarah went inside to the living room.

Sarah liked the fact that Surfer was used to running free in the house. It was only when she had given him to Michael that there was a problem. Michael would cry whenever he couldn't find his pet. It had led to a science project on rats that earned Sarah an A and provided a solution to keep Michael happy.

"Surfer needs a transmitter," Sarah had said.

Michael had looked at her like she was talking a foreign language. "A *what*?"

She had explained to him how park rangers track wolves and their cubs. The way they can locate bears. And panthers in the Everglades. A small transmitter that emitted an electronic signal. Sarah had gone on the Internet and found the perfect tiny transmitter and booster remote from a ranger in Florida's Alligator Alley. He had sent them to her, and she had attached the transmitter to Surfer's harness.

"Can I get the receivers?" Michael asked.

"Sure," Sarah said.

The receivers were a pair of small black boxes with meters and wire aerials on them.

"Is this good?" Michael asked, setting one of the meters on the living room floor.

"Sure," Sarah said. Michael turned the meter on and grabbed hold of the booster remote and pressed its single button. The remote was the size of a TV control, and when the button was pressed, it sent a signal that turned on Surfer's transmitter.

Michael tuned the receiver until the arrow of its meter pointed strongly in a single direction.

"He's *there*," Michael said, motioning toward the north side of the house.

"But where?" Sarah asked. "Where exactly?"

Michael tried to remember what Sarah had taught him to do next. He took the second meter and set it down a distance from the first. He tuned the receiver so its arrow also pointed in a fixed direction, too.

"Why don't we press the booster button more than once?" Sarah asked.

"Because it makes a spark. It makes a spark and it gives Surfer a shock."

"Right," Sarah said. "Very good. Now, what do you do to find Surfer?"

"Tri . . . tri . . . *triangulate*," Michael said, pleased he could retrieve the long, strange word.

"Exactly."

Michael put the booster remote on the coffee table and lay down on the floor. He wanted to be certain about the direction in which the needles were pointing. One arrow pointed toward the living room wall. The other arrow froze at an angle that, if projected by imaginary lines, would cross the first one somewhere beyond the living room.

"So, where is Surfer?" Sarah said.

"The arrows show the signal is coming from . . . from somewhere beyond the living room wall," Michael said. "From the backyard!"

"Right."

Sarah followed Michael out onto the rear patio. The door had a dog port from the home's first owners. Surfer had no trouble going in and out of the small swinging door. She watched Michael estimate that the arrows would cross down near the end of the lawn.

"Here," Michael said, running to the point where the grass met the asphalt seal.

Surfer was sitting at the mouth of a piece of rusty drain pipe and gnawing on a scrap of wood. Michael let out a whoop and picked up his pet.

"We're going to watch TV," Michael said, racing back into the house with Surfer. "He told me he wants to watch the news and a special on grizzlies and play Creature Feature on your laptop. He loves to dance to the background music."

"Tell me about it." Sarah remembered how Surfer had liked to watch her play Creature Feature from the very beginning. She started humming the song from her computer game. Surfer used to look like he was dancing to the music. He'd spin around, like a waltzing mouse, and sometimes she even used to get him to come in from the dump just by playing the music. Other times, the music made Surfer dreamy-eyed, and he'd take a nap.

For the first couple of years he seemed to like all the same computer games and TV shows she did, and listen to the Top Forty with her. Since Surfer had the transmitter on him, she always knew exactly where he was. He'd be in the backyard or running about on the dump. He was never gone very long. It was as if he'd disappear to hang out with the dump's rats, and then come back.

Sarah stayed out on the patio. It was almost five o'clock and the shadows from the huge asphalt mounds fell across the backyard. She dialed her father with the cell phone that she always wore clipped to the belt of her jeans. Her dad had bought the phone for her right after her mother's death, and insisted she keep it with her. He wanted to be able to call her at any time. He wanted to be able to know where she and Michael were and that they were safe.

"Hello." Her father answered the phone at his landfill office.

"Dad, it's me."

"Is everything all right?"

"Yes," Sarah said. "Can you come home soon?"

"I don't know when I'm going to get out of here," Mr. Macafee said. "Things are getting crazier."

"What else happened?"

"There were rats at White Water Park this afternoon," he said. "Kids on the water slides and in the main wave tank. Rats started coming out of the inflow pipes and drains. They were on the slides with the kids. Rats washing down the slides with little kids screaming. A couple of mothers fainted. I'm working with the police and the Health Department to contain it. We're flooded with phone calls. Rats in cereal boxes. Rats in people's beds. It's going to be on the news tonight and we're afraid of a local panic. I'll come home as soon as I can."

Since her mother died, Sarah had tried to understand the tension that crawled in her father's voice, even when he wasn't under pressure. There was always a special type of strain she'd noticed whenever he talked to her. Something in his voice that made her feel as though she never said the right thing. Maybe she was too anxious, that she was trying too hard to be something more than a daughter.

To look after him.

Like her mother had.

Maybe she *was* trying too hard to fill the emptiness her mother had left in all their lives.

"You and Michael should spend the night at Aunt Betty's," Mr. Macafee said.

"Dad, I don't think so," Sarah said. "We want to stay here and wait for you."

Sarah's aunt lived in Bayonne, a short ride across the Kill Van Kull. Sarah was used to taking their outboard, a fourteen-foot AquaSkiff with a two-hundred horsepower Johnson engine on the back. As long as Michael could bring Surfer, she knew he'd go.

"Are there rats in our house?" her father asked.

"No."

"If they're in everyone else's house, they're certainly going to be in ours. Watch out for them. They can fit through a hole as small as a quarter."

"We're not afraid of rats," Sarah said. It came out defensively, when what she had wanted to say was *Dad, we love you and we want to be here when you come home.*

When she hung up, Sarah heard Michael laughing. The channels on the living room TV were being changed rapidly. She looked in through the open patio window and saw Michael sitting on the sofa next to Surfer. Surfer was up on his haunches and poised over the TV remote. The long whiskers on his tiny white face were flicking excitedly, his nose twitching and sniffing at the air.

Michael was tickling him, but Surfer's small red eyes were glued on the screen. Michael pressed in the button for a channel. There was a rerun of a talk show. Surfer shook his head like he had a chill— like he didn't want to watch it. He pounced his front paws down onto the buttons of the remote, and a documentary on Komodo dragons flicked on the Science Channel.

Michael punched the talk show back on. Surfer shuddered again and hit the button for the Komodo dragons to come back. Michael giggled and saw Sarah watching them.

"He can't stand talk shows," Michael said.

Sarah laughed. The way Surfer's beady little eyes shifted from the TV to the remote made it look like he was really picking the programs. It looked weird, like something they should tape and send in to *Funny Pet Videos* or some program like that.

Sarah noticed that their next-door neighbors Mr. and Mrs. Hettle had come home. They were a young Indian couple with a six-month-old baby.

Their English was far from perfect, but they always had a smile and spent a lot of time tending to the squash vines they'd planted in their backyard. Sarah realized that they may not have heard about the rats.

"Hi, Hettles," Sarah called, starting across the lawn toward them.

They smiled at her. "Hello, Sarah," Mrs. Hettle said.

Sarah waited until she was closer. "Where's the baby?" she asked. They looked confused. Sarah mimicked rocking an infant in her arms. They understood and smiled again.

"She was tired when we came home. I gave her a bottle," Mrs. Hettle said. "She's having a nap."

They saw a look of concern crawl across Sarah's face.

"Did you hear about the rats?" Sarah explained. "The rats from the dump coming into the houses?" She could tell from the look on their faces that they didn't quite understand her English, didn't know what she was talking about. "You'd better check on her."

The Hettle baby girl lay in her crib enjoying the warm bottle of milk her mother had given her. She stared up at the glow-in-the-dark constellation and planet stickers her father had put on the ceiling, and she felt comfortable and sleepy. She let her eyes drift to the familiar faces of teddy bears and brightly dressed dolls and shadow puppets sitting on shelves, when something moved down by her feet. Something tickling, creeping up the blanket.

She tried to lift her head to see what it was, and for a few moments she expected to see the smiling face of her mother or father. Perhaps one of them was playing a game. They were hiding, tickling her with their fingers, and then they would appear above her and lift her up into their steady and safe arms.

For a while the baby thought whatever it was had gone away. She felt the wetness of milk clinging to her lips. For a few moments she closed her eyes and thought she would drift off to sleep. She waited for the pleasant feeling to grow, to spread across her chest and down to her legs. Her eyelids were heavy and starting to close, but the thing that was moving on top of her was closer now.

Something was near her neck.

There was a shadow, and then she saw a little face above her. It wasn't a doll. It wasn't anything she knew. It was a little brown twitching face with whiskers and small black eyes. A small hairy face—

and the baby began to feel afraid.

After a moment, she felt something on her chin and she could see the little face clearer now. The fur. The mouth. And its tongue gliding out from under two shining teeth. There came another little head next to the first.

Rats.

A pair of rats sat up on their haunches and began licking the milk from the baby's lips.

"Oh, God," Mrs. Hettle said, freezing at the doorway. Mr. Hettle started into the room past her, but Sarah caught him. Stopped him. Her instinct was for them to freeze, to not frighten the rats into doing anything sudden. Anything vicious.

The three of them stood still, the baby whimpering as the rats looked up from licking the baby's lips. They stared at the intruders. Sarah's mind raced through every book she had ever read about rats. Every program she'd ever seen. Every article and fact and rumor she'd ever come across. Her blood pounded in her chest, and she felt Mrs. Hettle trembling.

CHIRRRRR. CHIRRR.

Sarah recognized the chatter of a rat, the strange sort of squeaking sound rats made. But it was not coming from the rats at the baby's mouth. The sound was coming from behind her. They were louder, more urgent rat sounds than any she'd ever heard. Sarah and the Hettles turned toward the sounds.

CHIRRR. CHIRR.

Michael stepped through the doorway carrying Surfer on his palms.

"He's been making these sounds," Michael told Sarah. "He was freaking out. He wouldn't stop, so I wanted you to see . . ."

Surfer was staring straight at the dump rats, and he made the sounds again. He went up onto his haunches in Michael's hands. The dump rats appeared to be listening to the sounds. Understanding them. After a moment, the pair of dump rats turned away from the baby's mouth and ran along the edge of the crib.

Sarah and the Hettles moved toward the baby as the rats leaped on to the sill of an open window, their hindquarters shaking in a fast waddle. Sarah watched them jump into the backyard. A moment later, the last of their segmented, glistening tails had disappeared among the cloak of giant squash leaves and twisting vines.

5 • ENCOUNTER

"**W**as Surfer talking to them?" Sarah asked Michael as they crossed the Hettle's lawn back to their own house. "It looked like he was talking to the dump rats, telling them to skiddoo and leave the baby alone."

Michael didn't answer right away. "I don't know," he finally said. "He's been making sounds like that a lot lately."

They went in through the front of the house. "Surfer and I are going to play Dark Mountain and Creature Feature, and then watch a special on the difference between Nile and Australian crocodiles," Michael said, heading for the living room. Sarah paused in the foyer. The vision of the rats at the baby's mouth had burned its way into her brain. She felt creepy. Nervous. Her father's words haunted her. If rats had gone into so many of the other houses—if they had drunk from a crying baby's lips—then they could be anywhere.

"I'll bring you a 'slops.' We've got cream soda and I'll use scoops of fudge ripple," Sarah called to Michael, and she went into the kitchen. She halted in the middle of the linoleum floor and flicked on the bank of fluorescent lights on the ceiling. Her gaze moved over the L-shaped counter that fanned out from both sides of a deep aluminum sink, and stopped on the box of candy. She'd left it on the countertop when they'd come back from . . . Miss Lefkovitz. The top layer of candy bars had been disturbed. The wrapper on one had been ripped open, exposing the rich dark brown of chocolate. Whole chunks were missing.

"Did you eat any of the candy bars?" Sarah called out to Michael.

"Nope," his voice came back. "Can I?"

"In a minute."

The sun had started to sink behind the peak of the vast black mound behind the house. Its rays shot through the picture window that was sliced into the wall above the sink. *What do I do now?* Sarah asked herself. She thought about calling Michael in to show him what had happened to the candy, but he'd seen enough upsetting things for the day.

Perhaps Michael had nibbled on the candy, had ripped the wrapper and tinfoil underneath, and he didn't want to tell her. Perhaps he felt bad that he hadn't asked permission. If that was the case, it'd be a first. She checked the floor. If there were rats in the room, she wanted to know. "You're not taking over our kitchen," she said softly. "If any of you rats are here, you'd better clear out. Out."

Her eyes followed the wildflower trim of the white linoleum. She knew every inch of it from having swept it and mopped it a thousand times. The floor in front of the dishwasher was weak and buckled from several overflows that had soaked into the cheap plywood beneath. She had often wondered what lived down below the rotting, what was hiding beneath the linoleum cover and the wood. Were there termites? Wolf spiders? Large, hairy centipedes appeared from out of nooks and crannies in the summer and marched across the floor until they were destroyed by heavy doses of bug spray.

She thought she saw a movement in the space below the dishwasher. The machine had a black plastic front that had never been set to fit flush with the floor. The two or three inches of black void could shelter anything. There were plenty of places for rodents to hide beneath the washer and the stove. Once they found a family of mice that had come in for the winter and made a home in the stove. She remembered once when they'd made a roast chicken one Sunday. The smell of cooking mice was terrible. They had put down baited wire cages and spring traps and had to let the broiler burn for a whole weekend to get the stench out of the stove.

Sarah's attention returned to the candy box.

There were hiding places behind the lineup of appliances on the counter. She checked behind the blender and microwave. She moved a popcorn maker and heavy-duty juicer.

Nothing.

There were holes in the baseboard. Rats could come in through any opening that was as big as their skulls. There were holes that had been drilled for the thick electrical 220 cables that had to be brought in to power the oven. Her gaze came back to a black hole in the center of the sink.

A sound.

A sound from the blackness.

The garbage disposal. The black hole where they shoved the discarded trimmings of onions and carrots and the unwanted gristle from meats. The switch to turn the disposal on was on a slice of wall behind the sink. If rats were hiding in the black hole, she'd have to lean over and look into it.

Another sound.

"Get out now, you rats," she said. "*Now.*"

Her hands were shaking as she backed off and circled the floor trying to get a grip on her nerves. The sounds stopped. There's probably no rat in there, she told herself. If there were, it would have cleared now. It would have gone out the way it came in.

Instinctively, Sarah pulled open the storage drawer of the stove. There was nothing but a Dutch oven pot and its glass top. She stooped and tightened her grip on the transparent top, and lifted it like a gleaming shield. She held it in front of her face as she slowly straightened up and started toward the sink.

Her eyes were riveted on the black hole. She felt a pain in her chest, a tightening as she tried to hold the heavy glass top steady. She knew Norwegian rats—the kind of rats from the dump—could easily jump six to eight feet.

"I'm coming, you rats," she said, holding the shield at arm's length.

The floor creaked. The ice maker in the refrigerator made clinking noises as it dropped ice and its feeder gizmo changed positions. Each sound sent chills up the back of Sarah's neck.

"Are you there, rat?" she said, trying to lighten up. Her voice cracked. "It's me, Sarah."

Her throat tightened and she strained to see past the web of laser-sharp sun rays crashing in from the beveled window. Her belt felt crooked and tight against her stomach. She wanted to free up her hands to pull at her clothing, but she didn't dare set the shield down. She tried to laugh at herself for being so afraid.

A sound came from *inside* the disposal.

Something had moved in the black hole. A click, as one of the crude metal blades of the rotors was tripped.

Sarah leaned forward.

For a moment she thought she saw the back of a small animal, but it was the rubber wedges that safeguarded the top of the grinder. If there was a rat in the hole, she knew it could leap out. It could come fast, and sink its teeth into her neck. It could cut an artery.

Bite her throat.

Her face.

Fear wormed up into her jaws, and she felt her entire body begin to tremble. With the fear came a sharpness. Fast, quick thoughts. Her senses and instincts were drinking in everything in the kitchen. She was on high alert, like a panther.

An animal.

Quickly, she slammed the glass top down on the disposal. The eruption came suddenly. A shimmering brown bulk hurtling up from the black hole. The shrieking mass leaped up at her, hitting the shield. Sarah held down the glass top with all her strength, straight-arming the fat, raging rat like it was a flying football.

She was screaming as Michael ran in with Surfer. Michael saw her sister with her full weight against the glass lid. He saw the rat trying again and again to claw up past the cover.

"DOWN! DOWN!" Sarah yelled at the rat.

The rat fell down into blackness, and then hurled itself upward again. It knew it was trapped, and it pressed and shrieked desperately—horridly!—against the glass. The cover slipped a second, and the rat's front legs and claws burst out past the edges. A moment later, and its head was out from under the glass, too. The rat wiggled its body violently, a piece of stubborn life, a writhing thing that refused to halt or hide or stop.

Michael rushed toward the sink. Surfer screeched, made scolding sounds—as if he knew what was going to happen.

"Hit the switch!" Sarah cried. "Hit it!"

Michael's hand reached out over the snarling

head toward the wall switch, but his hand froze.

"TURN IT ON!" Sarah said.

Michael didn't move.

Sarah groaned and pressed solidly on the cover as she let one of her hands fly to the switch. She flicked it, and the blades of the disposal unit whirled.

The rat raged as it was pulled down into the hole. A second later, a single spray of its blood shot up high into the air and struck Sarah's face perpendicularly. She screamed at the hotness and cried out as the fluids of the ground rat dripped down her forehead and chin and onto the front of her blouse.

There was nothing pushing against the shield now.

Nothing as Sarah dropped the glass top. Michael yanked off a clutch of paper towels and thrust them toward his sister. She shuddered, took them, and cried as she wiped at herself madly. Michael hit the pump of the sink soap dispenser, wet a kitchen cloth towel, and began helping to rub soap and water on Sarah's face and neck and clothes.

Sarah wiped herself over and over.

Finally, her shaking stopped, and she pulled herself together.

"Pack your bag," Sarah said, gasping. "We're going to Aunt Betty's."

She and Michael ran up the half-flight to their rooms and threw their PJs, toothbrushes, and a few clean clothes into their backpacks. Sarah tried calling her father at the landfill offices, but the answering machine picked up, telling her to leave a message. Sarah knew her father was probably fielding one complaint call after the other. She knew he'd be busy for a long time, but he'd check his messages.

"Dad," Sarah said after the beep to speak, "call me when you get this message. There are rats in our house. We're driving the boat over to Aunt B's."

Michael put Surfer in his small traveling cage and caught up with Sarah at the back door after she'd closed all the drapes and blinds of the house. She noticed she'd missed a few drops of rat's blood on the sink cabinet, but she had no intention of doing any more cleaning now.

"Did you bring enough food pellets for Surfer?" Sarah said, programming the house phone for call-forwarding. She wanted all calls to come to her on the cell phone. "At least enough pellets for a week? Did you fill his water tube?"

"Yes," Michael said.

"Come on," she told Michael, heading out. She locked the back door behind them and led the way across the lawn to the asphalt. They crossed several hundred feet on the black tar surface to the landfill's marina gate. She'd taken the main set of house keys. Her father had marked the dump and marina key with a yellow plastic hood on the grip of the key. Only the handful of residents at Springville Gardens who had rented boat slips on Kull Creek could use the walkway to the pier.

They reached the narrow boardwalk that wove like a snake between the towering black mounds of the dump.

"It's getting dark," Michael said.

"We'll be out of here."

"Rats come out when it's dark."

Sarah looked at the graying sky over the Jersey factories. She thought they might have fifteen minutes or so before it would be night. The setting sun had already made the mounds into a moonscape. A bump marked where each of the thousands of small pipe vents had been covered in the clumsy rush to seal the dump. Sarah thought the few vents that had been left open would never be enough to handle all the methane generated by the rotting garbage.

There was a single duct with a twelve-foot

diameter, but it had nothing to do with ventilating the asphalt mounds. It was a fresh water drainage pipe that lead the several miles from Willowbrook Pond and traveled beneath New Springville and through the center of the largest mound to empty into the creek.

The noises of the night that filled Sarah with dread were louder out on the narrow boardwalk. Crisper. It had to be the gases from the dump, the hydrocarbons building up. Expanding. The walkway led through a trough between the two largest mounds of the dump.

A few hundred feet farther, they could see the dock at the edge of Kull Creek. Something was right about getting the outboard out of there and safely across the river to Aunt Betty's. Her father had finished paying the boat off. Her mother had loved traveling fast in the boat. They'd taken turns water-skiing. They fished for blues and gone on picnics together—and taken trips to Keansburg to ride the Whip and the Ferris wheel, and play the boardwalk games. They'd taken the boat to Sandy Hook. and Perth Amboy and the Tottenville beaches, and built bonfires to roast potatoes and sear hot dogs in the flames.

"The rats are coming," Michael said matter-offactly. "They're coming out."

He pointed below the narrow walkway.

Sarah saw the motion of the shadows beneath them. "There must be ruptures in the asphalt," she said. "They made the cover too thin."

"Rats can eat through asphalt," Michael said. "They can chew cement."

Sarah broke into a jog. "Hurry," she urged Michael.

She could see their boat, a white sixteen-footer, in its slip at the creek. She knew rats liked to chew wood, too, and she was afraid they might have already begun to eat through the wooden hull.

The rat sounds began.

CHIRRRR. CHIRRR.

Surfer made the sounds, too. His din was shriller. Disturbing. Like the squeals he'd made in the baby's room. Sarah and Michael were several hundred feet from the dock when they heard a tearing. A rumble. They felt the walkway sway as the earth moved behind them. The chattering of the rats was louder. Pulsing. Sarah and Michael looked back over their shoulders and stopped in their tracks. They saw more rats.

Many more rats.

"Oh, my God," Sarah said.

Michael began to tremble.

The mound beside them had split open. It was a monstrous wound, a wide crack about thirty feet long above the walkway. At first it appeared to be a small stream of oil or tar leaking out of the fracture. It took Sarah and Michael a moment longer to realize it was a current of large, glistening rats. Quickly, the dark living tide of rodents began to rise up onto the walkway behind them. It advanced like a colony of army ants across a plantation field, hundreds of rats scurrying atop the boardwalk and its railings.

A pack of rats moving toward Sarah and Michael.

Sarah turned Michael toward the marina, grabbed his hand, and pulled him along beside her. "Come on," she said, breaking into a jog.

CHIRRR. CHIRRR.

The torrent of rats below the boardwalk began to swell and widen in the trough like floodwaters filling an arroyo. There was another sound, a kind of muffled growling as if a wild beast were coming over the ridge above them.

"A truck!" Michael shouted.

Sarah saw the huge compactor truck loom over the top of the mound. The truck, its open top-bay grinding—crushing garbage—was closer than the boat. They recognized the driver. Marge Dixon was the only woman at the dump. She was a good driver, as strong and smart as any of the men. Marge would see them. She'd see Sarah and Michael, and she'd get them out of there.

6 • EXODUS

"**M**arge!" Sarah shouted. "Marge!" Marge didn't hear anything. She had her CD blasting, and the compactor on the five-axle truck was grinding up a load of fresh out-of-state garbage that she was taking out to the open tract. The blades and crushing arms scraped along the bed of the truck to stir the rotting waste, then rose on a conveyor gizmo to scoop the solids into the roaring teeth of the rear chipper. The police had delayed the work at the site. There had been a half-dozen men from the coroner's office picking over the area where Sabiesiak had gotten it. Marge felt uneasy about Leroy and what had happened to him. Uneasy? she thought. No. Downright creepy. She'd heard all they'd found of him was pieces. Mainly, a couple of his fingers.

Fingers.

The coroner had worn delicate white rubber gloves, and picked up the fingers and put them in a white porcelain washbasin. Marge hadn't seen the fingers, only heard about them from two of the other compactor/chipper drivers. Whatever, the delay pushed everyone into double-pay over-time, and at that rate Marge would work all night if they wanted her.

Marge threw the truck into low gear and started down the south slope of the asphalt mound. She scanned the sunset and creek. A love song was blast-ing over the din of the chipper. It was a lady cabaret singer that Marge liked a lot. The singer's voice always came straight from her heart, and she was warbling about some great guy that was driving a woman out of her mind, a song about remember-ing a lover: "*I think about you when the sun comes up. . . I think about you when I dim the lights . . .*"

Marge liked the singer a lot, because she was fat just like Marge was and they both painted over their lip lines so that they looked like they had larger mouths than they had. Marge often won-dered what the singer's cholesterol was and why she didn't have a personal trainer and cook, with all her money. Marge knew a lot of the guys in the Sanitation Department made jokes about her own weight. "Hey, here comes Large Marge," they'd say.

Or "Here's Marge. Lock up your lunch."

Marge pretended she never heard any of the cracks. "Worry about your own beer bellies," she'd growl under her breath, knowing she could knock most any of them out cold with a single uppercut if she wanted to.

Marge rolled her head and bellowed along with the song for a moment, then looked east and saw the two kids running on the narrow boardwalk. She recognized them straight off as being her boss's kids. The Macafee kids were nice kids. They'd always been respectful to her whenever she'd run into them at the office, and she used to baby-sit for them. The way they were waving their hands, they looked like they were in trouble.

Marge turned off the CD and compactor/chipper motors. The kids were shouting to her and pointing behind them to what looked like a flow of water—dark, oily water like the kind from the smelly creeks around the dump. It was dusk, and her eyesight wasn't that good. She'd meant to get new frames and lenses. The way the kids were running frantically, she was afraid that there was some sort of really bad danger.

A fantasy of saving Mack's kids leaped into her mind. She felt a weird flush of fear and excitement at the same time. The kids had probably gotten stuck out on the mound. It was getting dark and she came to the rescue. But the main roadway curved down and away from the boardwalk. She gave the truck the gas. Now—closer—she realized the darkness was not a flow of water.

It was something alive.

Then she understood what the kids were shouting.

"RATS! RATS!"

The realization of what was happening socked into Marge's brain like a spike. There was nothing she hated more than rats. Closer still, and she could see that the slick of rats was rising up beneath the boardwalk.

Rats on the railings.

Rats after the kids.

She knew she'd have to get to Sarah and Michael before the rats. Somehow, she'd have to get the truck down to them at the base of the mound.

"I'm coming!" Marge shouted out the truck's window. She accelerated, moved the truck along the high road above the walkway. She knew what she was doing was treacherous. The truck weighed nearly eight tons and it was carrying half a load. Eight tons of steel and machinery and gears and fuel. Just drive the truck, she told herself. Do it by the numbers. Stay on the roadway—the only part of the asphalt-covered mound that had been rein-forced to support the rumbling, giant juggernaut.

But the stream of rats was spreading fast. Marge saw the small fissures crackling up from the trough, shattering the base of the mound into a spiderweb. The rats were racing out. Marge knew she wouldn't have more than a minute or two to get the kids. She reached the parking lot of the marina, and turned the truck hard and fast.

Another fantasy flashed in her brain. Marge knew she would be in the *Staten Island Advance*. There would be a photo of her. WOMAN AT LANDFILL SAVES CHILDREN FROM RATS. The thought made her slam her foot down harder on the accelerator, racing to get the truck to the kids before the living tide. As the truck roared down beside the boardwalk, she thought she'd beat the rats. She saw the kids just ahead and began to sing. "*The coffee cup . . . I think about you . . . or am I losing my mind?. . .*"

She knew she wasn't getting the lyrics right, but it didn't matter. She was too nervous.

Frightened.

She drove along the edge of the scurrying tide of rats. For the first time she understood the urge that truckers have to run over turtles and possums and raccoons as they crossed highways. She'd been eating at truck stops when whole tables of truckers would laugh over stories of what kind of animals they'd hit, how they'd splattered a skunk or slammed into a deer and broke it in half.

I'll get you, she thought, letting the truck drift to the right until the front wheels smashed into the hordes of the rodents. She could hear dozens—hundreds!—of their bodies being squashed, saw their blood and juices flying out to the sides like she was plowing through a long puddle.

Suddenly, the left front wheel of the truck began to crack through and into the asphalt. A moment later, and the entire ground beneath the truck began to crack. Marge kept her foot on the accelerator. She kept the truck going, plowing forward like she was motoring through snow or thin ice. The drive wheels spun and whirled as the cab struggled and slowed, and, finally, ground to a halt. Another sound rose louder from beneath the cab, and Marge felt a chill shoot up her back.

CHIRRRRR. CHIRRR.

The kids kept running on the boardwalk toward Marge and the huge compactor truck. They realized that she had been trying to save them, but Surfer shrieked pathetically as they had watched Marge deliberately plow into the rats. She was trying to crush all of them. Through the windshield of the truck, Marge saw the flush of relief on the kids' faces change into expressions of terror.

The kids stopped. They were unable to help Marge now.

"She's made them angry," Michael said to Sarah. "Very angry."

Marge felt the truck beginning to vibrate. What looked like a wave of sludge rose up over the top of the grill. Dread swelled into Marge's chest and her throat tightened.

CHIRRRRR. CHIRR. CHIRR . . .

There was scratching.

Rapid, powerful scratching sounds on the outside of the doors of the truck. The scratching was like a bunch of keys being dragged along a blackboard. Marge's body quivered with the sound of rapid scraping and grating. She finally figured out what was happening, and threw her body across the seat to the passenger side. Her hand grabbed the window crank and she began to turn it urgently. She hollered as a shadow rose up on the window like a mechanical shade, and the first of the rats scampered in.

Marge grunted as she turned the crank faster.

Harder.

A few of the rats were caught between the rising

window and top of the frame. They shrieked, their eyes bulging and bursting as Marge's strength forced the window to cut them in half at their stomachs. Clawed legs were severed and dripped down the window in murky, scarlet fluids.

In her haste, Marge had bitten her own tongue. Shock and panic had made her slam her mouth closed and blood leaked through her teeth. By the time she'd turned to the driver's window, the rats were leaping into the cab by the dozens. Marge screamed and slapped at them with the flat of her hands, but they were racing about at her feet now. The cab floor rippled with wet fur and snarling small heads.

"Stop!" Marge cried out. "Please, God, stop!"

Several rats were inside her pants legs and climbing up her calves and shins. She felt their claws on her skin, digging in—then releasing. Digging in—and releasing. "Get off me! Get off!" She began to slap at her pants, to punch the squirming knots as they climbed. The dashboard was covered with the largest of the rats. They stared at Marge with small, mean eyes.

Marge threw up her arms, but the rats were already hurtling through the air toward her. They were ferocious beyond hunger as they landed on her head. Their claws dug in and began ripping the skin off of her face. Close-up, Marge thought the paws were like babies' hands, bald embryonic hands with shards of razors protruding from the fingertips. Her cheeks burned as if they'd been doused in acid. By the time her own hands reached her face, it was a mask of slimy wet fur. She grabbed the writhing small bodies that covered her eyes, and she yanked at them.

"EHHHHHH! EHHHH!"

She was in madness now, and Marge's right foot slammed down again to crush the accelerator. The tires howled, and somehow suddenly grabbed. The truck shot forward, crashed into the boardwalk, and headed straight for the kids. Marge's dreams of saving them were gone. There would be no Marge-the-Savior photo in the newspaper, she knew. Oh, she would be in the papers. Like Leroy Sabiesiak. She'd be in there just like Leroy.

The rats were tearing and biting the skin from the insides of her thighs. Several had crawled up her shirt and they bit vengefully at her naked arms and shoulders. In a moment, the rats had covered her face again. She felt the claws that tore into her eyeballs. She screamed as the paws scraped and bit into her sockets until the rats' teeth were at the gateway of her brain.

Marge was blind in her last moment alive. She grabbed the steering wheel and instinctively turned the truck away from the kids. Somehow it veered from crushing more of the walkway, and its tonnage roared up the side of the mound. If Marge had lived, she would have known the angle was too sharp. She had jackknifed a tractor trailer once on the New Jersey Turnpike. She knew when a truck was going over. With her dead at the wheel, the truck stalled like a climbing plane, then tumbled back down toward Sarah and Michael.

Michael had fallen as he turned to retreat. Sarah was half-dragging him along the boardwalk when the truck crashed into it. Sarah saw Marge's face. Saw the rats covering the cab and rats at her neck, digging into the side of her head.

The planking of the walkway split and tilted to throw Sarah and Michael sharply to the left. The wood snapped with a sound like rifle shots, jagged-edged splinters flying with the speed of shrapnel. Sarah held tight to her brother as they fell into the trough with its undulation of rats. Surfer shrieked as his cage hit the ground violently. The huge tires of the truck bore down toward them. Sarah didn't see Marge yank violently at the steering wheel. It seemed a miracle that the truck swerved away from them and began to climb up the side of the mound.

Gravity stopped the truck. Sarah was aware of it hovering above them on the slope. She knew it was still in motion. Not stable.

Balancing.

Michael was on his feet next to her. He grabbed Surfer's cage, and Sarah pulled him with her, wading through the shattered wood and panicking rats. For a moment she thought about turning back, but the boardwalk had buckled into a perpendicular wall. The only way was forward, to get beyond the ruptured planks and climb back up on the walkway. The monstrous length of the truck hovered fifty feet up the right slope of asphalt, and already its front wheels were turning back down toward them.

Sarah cried out as she saw the truck listing. A moment later, the cab angled back down the slope, and she saw Marge, her face hardened into a ghastly grimace. The enormity of her body fell forward like a fat, graceful clown. In death, she tumbled easily, her full weight crashing down onto the center bank of levers that controlled the truck's special motors.

There came a growling and roaring as the compactor and chipper engines came alive once more.

The truck was tilting now, inch by inch, as it crunched the asphalt like a tank on ice.

Michael stopped suddenly, standing ramrod straight and still clutching Surfer's cage. Sarah's breath burst from her in short, awful gasps as the truck slid and tumbled toward them. The splitting asphalt made a deep, ripping sound, and its wheels caught for a moment on a row of feeble vent pipes.

Sarah made a last attempt to get Michael clear, but the body of the truck was airborne now, falling over. She grabbed Michael's hand and got an arm around his waist as the truck flipped onto them. She waited for the crushing death of its steel.

Waiting . . .

Waiting.

But when she opened her eyes, she saw that *somehow* she and Michael were *inside* the truck's inverted garbage chamber. They were trapped in the stench of its roaring bowels.

The truck shook like a huge, furious turtle on its back, and the upside-down conveyor blades scraped along the ground toward them. The putrid smell of the chamber tore into Sarah's nostrils, and she struggled to see in the scant light from the drainage holes that were now like so many stars on the fetid ceiling. She and Michael were waist-deep in trash.

Michael clutched Surfer's cage. Sarah grabbed her brother's hand.

"Watch out for the scoop blades!" she cried.

The garbage lifted into waves as the blades beneath them advanced. They had to jump over the blades like they were playing a nightmare game of jump rope.

CRAAAANK.

"What's that?" Michael asked.

Sarah saw the metal wall at the back of the chamber begin to move toward them. Michael looked to her. Hydraulic pistons had activated the compactor. "We have to get out or we'll be crushed!" Sarah shouted over the din of motors. "Or be fed to the chipper!"

Sarah pulled Mike away from the advancing steel wall. The scoop blades beneath their feet churned up several larger sections of plank from the shattered walkway. "We have to stop it," Sarah cried, grabbing a piece of board and trying to jam it into the roof of turning gears.

The plank disintegrated and the chipper began to whirl. A first wave of garbage had triggered the feeder. Michael spotted a piece of pipe. He shoved it into the gears, but the gears chewed it, too, like it was a thin plastic tube.

Sarah had always watched the huge trucks—her father took her for rides in them, let her know about all the machinery and tools and motors at work. She had asked questions like a boy, and he had been proud of her. She remembered noticing that the compactor/chippers each had a cab with a special rear window. It was glass and had a steel cover that dropped into place when the compactor was in use.

"HELP ME!" Sarah cried, wading through the garbage toward the front. "IF WE CAN GET INTO THE CAB, WE CAN SHUT EVERY-THING OFF."

She and Michael reached the steel cover as the rear wall rumbled closer, sifting and packing the garbage. The larger chucks of debris were pulled into the screaming teeth of the chipper. Sarah pressed her hands against the wall, feeling for the cab's window. She felt the slime and crust of months of filth and decaying garbage. Her fingers clawed down to the rivets, and she tried to remember the truck was upside down. It was upside down. Would the partition cover and window be higher?

Lower?

She was trembling. Confused.

Michael freed up both his hands by climbing on top of the garbage and wedging Surfer's cage against the wall with his knee. He felt the slime, too.

"Jeez," he said, sickened.

"What?"

He lifted his hands up into the scattering of light from the drainage holes. His palms were covered with small white worms—maggots!—growing in the sheath of rotting lard and gristle. The truck shifted again, and the feeble light spread so the whole of the chamber's walls were glimpsed to be a blanket of worms and larvae. Sarah gagged and tasted a trace of vomit that rushed up from her stomach.

"Where is it?" she cried. "Where's that *window*?"

Together they found the ridge of the partition cover and forced it down to expose the glass. They could see Marge's body and a wash of rats dashing about confused, heading out through the cab windows.

Sarah banged at the glass. It was thick.

Reinforced with wire.

Michael found a piece of vent pipe. He began hammering at the glass, but it wouldn't give. Sarah took the pipe and started to thrust it like a spike.

Hard.

Harder.

The glass shattered and fell away like glistening specks from a broken windshield. Michael was the only one small enough to fit through the window, and Sarah hoisted him up. He began to cry as he reached past Marge's bloodied, dead face toward the bank of control levers.

"Higher!" he yelled.

"I can't." Sarah's voice came from behind him.

"Lift me *higher*!"

Michael saw Marge's raw and scarlet cheeks begin to move. He choked as her mouth twitched and swelled as if she were rolling her tongue and going to laugh.

"Oh, God," Michael cried, as a mucus-covered rat wiggled its way out from between Marge's lifeless lips. The sight of it made him hurl himself forward until he punched at the levers with all his might.

The motors stopped.

Died.

Sarah pulled him back into the bed of the truck. They dug down into the garbage until they could crawl out through a space beneath the stalled blades of the conveyor. Somehow they were in the twilight again and scampering back up onto the boardwalk. They were running—with Surfer in his cage—running with their life away from the truck and Marge and the raging stream of rats.

7 • TRANSGRESSION

"Why didn't they bite us?" Sarah gasped as she and Michael reached the marina. "Why'd they kill her? They killed Marge, not us. Why?"

Michael was already ahead of her, racing out onto the pier. There was no time for words. He scampered onto their AquaSkiff, peeling back its canvas cover. Surfer was still shrieking as he set him and his cage down in the bow. He checked the red-painted cans that were the gas tanks and began to pump the fuel-line bulb to prime the engine.

Sarah grabbed the front tie rope and threw it free of its piling. She raced to the stern and stopped before untying the final rope. She needed to think. Was there something else they could do? The cell phone. She remembered the phone. She tried dialing her father, but her hands were shaking and the number buttons too small. When she finally got the number in correctly and pressed the SEND button, there was a busy signal.

"Hurry," Michael yelled. "The rats are still coming."

The fissures of the mound had spread to the marina, and the stream of rats began to flow off the bank and into the water. The splashes came slowly at first, like a pan of popcorn when it starts to pop. The splashing sounds came faster—faster!—until the main flow of rats began to pour into the creek. Rats were piggybacking, in some places three or four on top of each other, as they dropped.

Michael yanked the start cord of the engine. Nothing happened.

The rats began to form a rippling, expanding wedge on the surface of the water. The shape looked like an area of turbulent water or a strong wind rustling up a cat's-paw. The disturbance began to spread toward them on the boat. Sarah threw off the final rope and jumped into the boat.

"Let me try," she said.

Sarah checked the gas level in the bubble window at the top of the main gas tank. She moved the throttle from neutral into forward, and then back again. The wave of swimming rats began to close on the boat. She heard them scraping the sides, clawing to climb up into the boat.

Michael already had the emergency paddle. He slapped it at the water, trying to sweep the rats off the side planking. Only a handful of them had made it into the boat by the time the engine roared to life.

"Sit down!" Sarah yelled to Michael.

She threw the throttle wide open. The prop of the outboard screamed as it bit into the water and threw a wake of bubbles and oil out behind the boat. Sarah sat behind the wheel, flicked on the head and safety lights, and steered the boat away from the pier. Michael scooted about after the few rats in the boat with a fishing net. He caught them one by one and dropped them into the black oil-slicked water. Strings of lights came on suddenly across the huge mounds of asphalt. Crude streetlights lined the main roads linking the mounds. Sarah slowed the boat. She didn't want to run into any flotsam, planks of wood, or tin cans and bottles—anything that could shatter the cotter pin of the prop. The last of the twilight made the Jersey side of the river surreal. Factory lights burned brightly. Smokestacks coughed forth tremendous white streams of smoke, ghostly fingers reaching high into the blackening sky. The tops of the refinery chimneys shot out flames and ripples of yellow sulfur. Circles of light marked the several platforms that clung to the enormous Staten Island Con Ed plant.

"Watch out for the containers!" Michael yelled.

Chains of long plastic cylinders designed to restrict oil spills undulated like green snakes on the surface of the creek. Sarah stood up behind the wheel checking the mazelike path for the exit to the Kill. The final stretch took the boat beneath high tension wires. In the distance to the north were the neon lights of a car dealer, a cinema center, and a health club. On the left bank, several of the mounds looked like the huge sprawling salt domes of Texas. Telephone poles stuck out of a ridge like giant crucifixes, and snow fences were silhouetted against the sky for as far as they could see.

A lone young man sat in a rowboat just off the largest of all the mounds.

"It's Hippy!" Michael said.

Hippy was the nickname all the kids had given to the man watching his crabbing lines. He was like the town idiot, dreadlocked brown hair that hung down his back. He lived alone in a dilapidated frame house on the Arthur Kill at the end of Sandy Lane. The rumor was that his mind had been baked out on drugs, and he always yelled like a maniac at kids and freighters and seagulls for scaring away fish from his lines and raiding his crab traps. No one else along the whole creek touched anybody's crabs or fish, because of the pollution. The waters were restricted and all fishing was illegal anyway.

Sarah checked the wake behind the skiff. Rats were still dropping from the banks into the creek, and the cat's paw began to boil.

"We have to warn him," Sarah said.

Hippy turned his angry, bearded face toward them at the sound of the motor. "KEEP AWAY! KEEP AWAY!" he screamed at them, waving his hands like he was sending semaphore. He had on his usual ripped overalls and a sweat-stained denim shirt.

"Hey, mister, there are rats!" Michael called. "Rats."

"Rats in the water," Sarah joined in.

"Keep your boat away!" Hippy screamed. "Away! You're scaring the crabs! You're scaring them!"

Suddenly, Hippy raised a shotgun and aimed it at them.

"Hey!" Michael yelled.

Sarah turned the skiff away from the rowboat.

"Everyone says he never has the gun loaded," Michael told Sarah. "He just makes believe."

"Well, we're not going to find out," Sarah said. She saw Hippy put down his gun. She eased off on the throttle and circled between Hippy and the swimming swarm of rats. "Mister," she called to him. "There really are rats swimming toward you. They've hurt people. Bitten them. They killed someone."

There was a sudden shudder that Sarah and Michael felt in the boat. A jolt, like Sarah imagined an offshore earthquake would feel. A new sound crept into their consciousness, a low, deep rumbling. For a moment Sarah was baffled. She thought the mounting vibration, the sound that seemed like they were near a giant woofer speaker, might be her father. Her dad and other workers in trucks, rescuers coming for them. They might have seen them, like Marge had, while patrolling the grounds. A night wind had sprung up and rushed across her face as she looked toward . . .

The sound was coming from the mound.

Hippy, too, could hear the rumble. Sarah stared at his silhouette as he stood in his rowboat and faced the black cliff that rose from the creek bank. Her instinct was to flee, to turn the boat toward the Kill and escape the watery labyrinth. They'd be out on the open river and heading for Aunt B's. They'd see the lights of Bayonne, and in ten or fifteen minutes—in no time at all—they'd be having hot cocoa and Aunt B would make their beds and they'd be watching her thirty-two-inch TV.

CRACK. CRAAACK.

There was new motion now. Something moving. A flux that held Sarah and Michael riveted. They stared astonished as the mound face in front of Hippy began to split open with a roar. Not the sparse and weblike splintering of the trough and the boardwalk. The largest of the mounds cracked wide, a vast fissure starting at the top and violating the full six or seven stories of its height. Massive chunks of the asphalt facing gave way, dropping into the creek like the crumbling side of an iceberg. The entire mountain opened, a monstrous pop-out Epiphany card, exposing a vast slab of the complex and oozing interior.

Sarah and Michael stood transfixed. At first, Sarah could only grasp the tremendous glistening and infinite tiering. There was level upon level of irregular compartments and tunneling, as if someone had taken an ax and chopped away the front of a massive hive of termites or bees. But instead of insects, hundreds—thousands!—of rats shimmered and moved like ghastly images in an intricate tapestry. The megalopolis of rodents appeared suspended in shock for a moment, then began to fracture and drop. Rats rained down from the heights, splashing, dropping into the creek.

"Get out of there!" Sarah screamed at the young man.

Michael looked down at Surfer shrieking in his cage. It was as though Surfer knew exactly what was happening. Michael looked back to the rowboat. "They'll bite you!" he yelled to Hippy. "They'll kill you!"

The first wedge of swimming rats reached the skiff. "We have to get him," Sarah told Michael. She eased the throttle forward to keep the skiff in front of the rats that had followed them down the creek. As she motored toward the rowboat, the full dimensions of the freakish rat city hit her. Swells of rats pulsated from the greasy bowels of the mound, rats falling in a dark, curdling cascade. Severed tunnels appeared to be long, elaborate balconies that dripped with rats. Rodents raced insanely down perpendicular shafts. Masses of rusty and putrefied debris appeared like macabre altars and horrible faces.

For a moment Sarah thought they would reach the young man in time. But he stood in the rowboat with his back to them and ignored their cries. They were less than fifty feet from him when the first boiling wave reached him.

Sarah thought the young man would row away. He had begun to pull up the anchor and his crab traps. The oars were in the locks. He could have sat down on the center seat and plunged the oars into the water. He could have rowed toward them and made it to their skiff.

Instead he seemed to be waiting.

The water in front of him bubbled and churned. As the rats reached the rowboat there was a sudden wall of massive turbulence. The boat was hit with white water, as though the creek had become a river with treacherous rapids. The whiteness swelled over the side of the boat and then turned dark as the front line of rats gushed up onto the boat. The surge capsized the boat, plunging the young man into the water.

"No!" Sarah yelled, pushing the throttle forward. By the time they reached the swarm of rats Hippy had disappeared beneath the surface.

Sarah reeled as she turned the boat in circles in the open water between the two closing swarms of rats. The spiral of the wake kept the rats from climbing onto the boat. Where Hippy had gone under was now a violent disturbance, as if an enormous school of piranhas were making a kill. Sarah crossed the spot a dozen times. Michael struck out with the paddle, hoping there was something they could do.

Something.

"He's gone," Sarah said finally. "He's gone."

Here, closer, the huge ruptured mound appeared to be a hideous earthen temple. The stench of death and decay socked into their nostrils. The flux of wet slimy rat bodies took on phantasmagoric shapes, like tea leaves in a gypsy's cup. Whole clumps of rats crawled on the face of the fissure, plummeting, creating nightmare shapes of beasts and monsters and demons. The sounds of the rats became throbbing, pulsing, an ungodly chant.

"Oh, my God," Sarah said.

She stared at a motion in the water. A face had surfaced and appeared to be looking at them.

"It's Hippy," Michael cried out.

At first, Hippy's head was above the water, his eyes open, and Sarah expected at any moment he'd wave to them. Perhaps he was a great swimmer, she thought. Perhaps there had been a sudden undertow, an astonishing current that had swept him clear of the rats and he was able to hold his breath for a very long time. Perhaps he had swum toward the shore.

But he was emerging in the deluge of rats. Sarah

saw his shoulders now, and the rest of his torso as it levitated straight out of the water. Hippy began to scream.

"He's alive!" Michael said.

"The rats have him—don't look!"

Michael began to hyperventilate, to breathe fast and hard, and gasp. Sarah pulled him to her, turned his head away from the grotesque sight. Hippy's eyes were open. He appeared to be paralyzed, except for his throat. His scream. The rage and terror in his eyes. He was being carried up into the shadows of the bank. His whole body was out of the water now, rising up the face of the fissure. He rose headfirst, his arms stretched out and rigid. Clumps of his hair were pulled taut, like astral rays bursting from his skull. Hundreds of rats were moving him, lifting him—transporting him upward like ants dragging a large crust of bread up a hill. An aura of rodents held him in his teeth, clawing their way with their burden, up higher.

Higher.

"God," Sarah said. She saw new movement from the shadows of the fractured mound. There were black forms emerging from an overhang. These rodents were two and three times larger than the others. An inner sanctum of shocking, gargantuan rats, rats like she'd only read and heard about in TV news reports about Chile and Argentina. Fatted, perhaps mutant rats from the nitrate mines and toxic dumps. Huge rats that were now common-place in the streets of Santiago and Buenos Aires.

The rats that were transporting Hippy released their hold on him. Several of the largest rats raced out from the darkness and began to sniff at the screaming prey. Hippy's cry was shrill now, beyond dread and astonishment and horror. Still his body lay paralyzed. Sarah saw the flash of huge gnawing teeth as the chorus of rats from the mound made frantic new sounds. Sounds like monkeys make in a jungle forest when their head monkey is arriving. Sounds of fear and obeisance and terror.

At a signal from the largest rats, the horde rushed the young, screaming man. Quickly—riotously!—they began to feed on him.

8 • THE KILL

When the call came from his daughter, Mack Macafee felt a relief that only a man who had been living under the specter of a wife's death could know; a relief born of the constant fear that somehow Death would find its way into his life again. That God or the Devil or whatever made the world tick would somehow scheme to take his children, too, away from him.

"Where are you?" Mr. Macafee had asked Sarah, lifting his hulking frame from his desk.

"Heading north on the Arthur Kill. We'll be safe at Aunt Betty's," Sarah had yelled into the cell phone over the din of the outboard.

Sarah had poured out to him everything that had happened. The largest mound cracking open. Rats surging and leaping into the Fresh Kills. The attack on Marge. Hippy. Sarah cried out everything through tears and gasping and fright. She and Michael were safe in the boat. The swarm of rats were far behind them now, just boiling out of the dump's creek and into the Kill.

"You stay with your aunt," Macafee had ordered.

"Stay in the house. Keep away from her dock and the Kill."

"Okay, Dad."

The waterway disturbed Sarah. The rats. The stench of the air. The death and horror that they'd seen at the landfill. All of the terrible things that had happened seemed logical now in this drab, exhausted place. People had ruined the water and the land and the air for as far as she could see. Oil-and-grease-covered barges lined a dead black shore. Everything was endangered. Crawling. Dying.

As senseless as their mother's death.

Sarah kept turning, staring behind at the wake, expecting to see the tide of rats. She knew they wouldn't be able to swim as fast as the boat, but the thought of them made her skin crawl. She no longer trusted anything.

She knew the main tide of rats could have crossed the channel and decided to infest the rotting warehouses and barges in Carteret. South was the ocean and Sandy Hook. But there were the small rat colonies even here along the Kill Van Kull. Perhaps the main swarm would come north. They'd seethe on the surface like a spawning, and probably disperse into the main bay.

A chill shook her body and she decided not to

think about such things anymore. She'd think about her father. Her father in trouble. That was who she had to worry about.

Macafee had his head thrust forward. The fluorescent light above him made his freckles a deep, vivid orange. He had already heard about the rumbling, the failure of the mounds. Reports had come in from other sanitation workers in the field. They had found Marge's truck and what was left of her body. They saw that the face of the largest mound had crashed down into the creek. Thousands and thousands of rats were still rushing into the water. The boiling covered the whole of the Fresh Kills waterway, and the first of the swarm had reached the Arthur Kill.

John Medina, Macafee's assistant, had reported from the site. From the highest secure ridge, Medina could see the lights of his boss's office a mile off to the south. The office building was a rusty rectangle about the size of a barn, with sides and a roof of corrugated tin. The fence around the entire dump there was as high as a prison's, and it was topped around the equipment areas with dripping curls of razors and barbed wire.

"Any sign of the hippie?" Macafee had asked.

"Not yet."

"What happened? Was it the gas? The methane? Did the gas from the garbage crack open the mounds?"

John had pulled his Mets cap on tight, and wore a sweat jacket over his T-shirt. He walked to the edge of the main drop-off where the major section of the asphalt had fallen away from the highest mound. He saw the gnawing marks. The signs that furious, desperate digging had taken place to undermine the asphalt. "Let's say the rats probably didn't appreciate being gassed," John said. "It looks like they didn't like it at all. Couldn't breathe it. It was probably a case of survival for them."

Captain Nagavathy was mooring his tuna trawler *Parsifal* off Sheepshead Bay just after midnight when he heard about the rats on the Coast Guard frequency. He'd had a disappointing run off Montauk. The schools of tuna had thinned at a time when he'd invested his entire life's savings into the *Parsifal*. It had state-of-the-art equipment for harvesting large runs of fish, hauling them aboard in crank nets, and a complete automation to process, control-portion size, and can them right aboard. A crew of five men was all he needed. The *Parsifal* was designed to pay for itself in four years.

His first mate stopped by his cabin. "I'm turning in for the night, Captain."

"Right, Radman," Nagavathy said.

Radman said, "Something will turn up. By tomorrow night we ought to run into a good school, at least blues or strippers, probably before we hit Provincetown. Don't worry."

But Captain Nagavathy *was* worried. Half the tuna boat and fishing fleet owners in the Northeast were worried. The mortgage on the boat was late. His son was in California trying to get a job directing commercials, and Nagavathy had to pay his phone and car lease bills. His daughter, just a few months out of Wesleyan, needed rent and food money. As it was, all he could afford for her was a cramped apartment on 185th Street in Washington Heights and a small allowance.

He opened himself a can of cheap beer and moved closer to the ship-to-shore. He caught a glimpse of himself in the mirror. His shock of prematurely gray hair. Cheeks vein-broken from high blood pressure and windburn. And the drinking. The report of rats swarming in the Kill absorbed him. He was always one to add things up. Hear about the rats, get the idea, man. If the Coast

Guard was worried about the rats, then somebody would be pretty grateful if there was a way to get rid of them. If they'd be grateful at the right price, the *Parsifal* would be able to do the job. His boat could net the rats, process them, turn them into fertilizer or cans of dog food—or whatever they wanted.

Nagavathy sat at the radio preparing to open the channel to the Coast Guard. He played what he'd say in his head first. It would sound like an unusual pitch, he knew, but it made sense.

The Parsifal's designed for harvesting fish. You've got a rat problem. You've got to use imagination.

We're a big operation. We could scoop up a sizable colony of swimming rats. Drop them onto our conveyors. We're automated. We can set the on-board cannery to grind them, chop up the product. Even package them. Sure, we usually catch tuna for human consumption. Label the cans and they're ready for the supermarket.

Can we clean the machinery? Of course. The Board of Health allows for a percentage of rodent parts per each can. They know that tuna ships have a few rats aboard. There's always one or two of them dropping into the choppers by mistake and ending up in somebody's stuffed tomato or sandwich. It's not a big deal. Every can of tuna fish in the supermarket has rat hairs and vermin bone

fragments in it. Cockroach legs. Pieces of spiders. You got
everything in there. Just like in hot dogs.

Sarah kept the throttle open, bringing the skiff up
to near thirty miles an hour. The Fresh Kills Creek
emptied into the Arthur Kill across from Carteret.
They were north of Travis and Pralls Island. Aunt
B's would be beyond the narrows of Elizabethport
and Howland Hook.

"More rats!" Michael shouted from the bow. He
held Surfer's cage on his lap and pointed toward the
Staten Island shore. The cloud cover had broken
and a bright yellow full moon rose in the sky over
Newark Bay. Sarah saw a small cluster of rats at the
base of the pilings of an old pier. They lingered at
the tide line where patches of mud and oil had collected and congealed over several years.

"What are they doing up here?" Sarah said. One
of the rats was huge, at least two feet in length plus
its tail. "It must be an isolated family. They must
have come up from the mounds days, weeks,
before."

On the south bank of the bay they saw a couple
of other colonies under the pier lights, and a fourth
was seen as they headed east through the Kill Van
Kull. That was the way the waterways connected.

The dump creek into the Arthur Kill into the Kill Van Kull.

They saw Aunt B's dock and Bayonne coming up past Uncle Wiggly's amusement park. Aunt B, in jeans and a flowered smock, was already out at the end of her dock waving to them.

9 • VOICES

"**Y**our father called," Aunt B said, as she caught the bowline and tied the skiff up next to her own sleek, moored inboard. "I know about the vermin. The rats. My God, poor Marge Dixon and that demented hippie man. I knew Marge. She and I used to talk whenever I was visiting your father at the dump. She used the same arthritis doctor I do at St. Vincent's, and we went to the same church for a while. Our Lady Star of Christians. What a terrible thing."

"It was pretty gruesome," Sarah said, helping her brother get his things onto the dock. Michael carried Surfer in his cage.

"And it was gross, too," Michael said.

Aunt B gave them each a big hug and started brushing off their clothes with her hand. "You certainly look like you've been in a garbage truck. And smell it. Baby Jesus, you could have been killed." She took Michael's backpack and slung it over her left shoulder. "Let's get you both a nice hot soak and something to eat," she said, as she started toward the isolated small frame house across the street from the line of private docks with their whitewashed pilings.

Aunt B was bent and overweight, and used a shiny aluminum cane. Her voice was loud and strong, and her bright blue eyes shone out from her China-doll haircut. "Your father said something about them bringing in a tuna trawler to clean them up," Aunt B said, opening the front door. "Net the rats. Get rid of them."

"A trawler?" Sarah said. "There are too many rats. Billions of them."

"Zillions," Michael said.

"I'm sure it looked that way," Aunt B said, closing the door behind them, and headed straight for the kitchen. "He's got the Coast Guard in on it, and they're already calling up the Fort Wadsworth unit of the National Guard. Police helicopters. Professional exterminators. He said we shouldn't even try to get through to him. He'll call us. I don't understand how rats killed Marge if she was driving one of the big compactor trucks. What happened?"

"You don't want to know."

"Well, you can tell me after you've had a glass of hot cocoa. You guys jump in the tubs, and then we'll make waffles with maple syrup and Ben and Jerry's ice cream."

"Great," Michael said. He put down Surfer's cage on the wide shelf of the breakfast nook window, got a handful of food pellets, and put them into the cage. Surfer was silent now, sitting up on his haunches and looking at them.

Sarah caught a reflection of herself in a mirror. She ran her fingers through her hair. Its tangled brown strands hung straight to her shoulders, and she tried to brush out what looked like pieces of dried food and scraps of paper. The mirror had a copper frame hammered with sailors' knots. All the Macafees were water people, had been raised on boats, and Aunt B kept up with her 280-horse-power watercraft inboard. Before she'd lost her husband to cancer, the two of them would catch up with her brother and the kids at Sandy Hook or Barnegat Lighthouse for beach-bumming and volleyball.

Aunt B poured the hot milk into mugs, each with a packet of cocoa and miniature marshmallows. She sliced several pieces from a pan of banana bread, spread them with cream cheese and raspberry jam. After their dinner and baths, Aunt B led them in a short prayer for their father and asked, "Want to play cards? How about Pig or Floating Queen poker?"

"Pig," Michael said.

They played at the card table in the living room and kept the large-screen TV on in the background. The rats barely had a mention on the Channel 4 news. The newscaster made reference to a sinkhole opening up at the Staten Island landfill, and that some of the local residents had to be evacuated because a few rats were in the sewer system. There was no mention of Marge or Leroy or Miss Lefkovitz—or the methane vents. Nothing about anyone dying or the staggering mass of rats that had broken out into the Kill Van Kull.

At 7:00 P.M. Michael switched the channel to the local cable station. There was coverage of a high school baseball game, and a middle school quiz show called *The Cranial Crunching*.

"There's Dad," Sarah said, suddenly pointing to the screen. The picture was of a group of men, some in suits, walking swiftly along near the edge of a fractured mound. She and Michael dropped forward onto the carpet for a closer look. Aunt B sipped her cup of cocoa and stood behind them. "I told him to pray," she said.

The image cut away from the men to flickering lights in the night sky. The police helicopters circled above the dump, scanning the ruptures in the asphalt.

Michael let out a cry of joy at a closeup of his father, but Sarah could see their dad was exhausted. Worried. She didn't like the way everyone was after him, cornering him. Reporters were in his face with questions: *Is it true the dump was sealed? Methane's a flammable gas, right? Couldn't the dump have blown up? Houses explode? The whole place could detonate, right? Where are the rats? Rats carry bubonic plague. The fleas. It's the fleas that kill you, is that what it is? Where are the rats swimming to?*

Where?

"We have everything under control," Macafee told the reporters. But Sarah could hear and see that he was worried. Confused.

Drained.

"Everyone clear out," a young man in a Mets cap was shouting into a bullhorn. John Medina was running interference for his boss like he usually did. The reporters began to shove the microphones into Medina's face.

"We heard that the rats killed someone," a young woman reporter said. The handheld TV camera tried to follow the action, but Macafee and his men were heading for a squadron of panel trucks and SUVs.

"We're evacuating the area," Medina shouted

into the bullhorn. "The rats are gone from the land-fill. There's nothing more to see here. There was an infestation at the dump. A few rats got in the houses. The rats are all gone now."

Sarah stood up next to Aunt B. "What's Dad doing?" she asked. "Where are they all driving to?"

"He told me they were moving the command post away from the dump."

"Command post?" Michael said. "What is this? A *war*?"

Aunt B hesitated before answering. "Your dad said they'd work out of offices in the old Stapleton Pier Six on the bay. He says nobody knows exactly what the rats are doing. They don't know where they're swimming to. He said he hasn't been able to find anyone for the whole operation who knows anything about rats. There's some woman at the Museum of Natural History, but even she doesn't know anything about rats on this scale."

Michael took Surfer and his cage up to his cousin's room. Aunt B's son, Charlie, was twenty-eight now, living in Baltimore and married to a nurse, but Aunt B had kept his room the same as when he had moved out. Michael loved Charlie's old room with its own TV set and Nintendo games.

Sarah got her cousin Janice's old room. When

Sarah had an important school paper to write or needed private space away, she could count on Aunt B coming to get her and putting her up in Janice's old room. She'd put a lot of her rat research on Janice's old laptop computer, she remembered. Even all the computer games like Creature Feature and Beam Wars. The laptop was practically an antique, no faxing or other frills, but it worked fine for word processing and data storage. She opened the laptop and turned it on.

I know about rats, she said to herself. She wished her father would have remembered. She wished he had thought of that.

Thought of her.

She'd gotten a lot of mileage out of having a rodent for a pet. Term papers. Science fairs. The rat folders came up on the laptop screen. For a moment, she fantasized that her mother was somewhere in the room with her.

Alive.

She'd be saying, *Yes, Sarah, look for something to help your father. You know more about rats than any museum or zoo or . . .*

Help him, Sarah.

Help him.

Aunt B peeked her head in after the ten o'clock

news. "You must be whacked out," Aunt B said.

"I can't sleep," Sarah said.

"I know," Aunt B said. "Just the thought of rats makes my skin crawl. I was thinking how they're just what Staten Island and New Jersey need: another pestilence. It's like the end of the world around here. All the factories and the poisons in Cancer Alley. Everything dying. Now, packs of rodents. What's next? Locusts?"

It was ten-thirty before Sarah shut off the computer, put out the lights, and lay down. She didn't want to watch any of the talk shows or comedians. She let the background waltz music for Creature Feature play. *LA DA DA DUM, LA DEE DA DA, DA DUM ...*

The weirdest facts about rats from the computer files raced through her mind:

Rats move along walls by using the vibrissae, whiskers on either side of their face. Pet rats leave droppings and urine on their owners. Wild rats can kill poultry, lambs, and baby pigs. . . .

Sarah remembered the sounds she'd heard when the rats were at the Hettle baby's mouth.

CHIRRRRR. CHIRRR.

Later—finally—she fell asleep, and even then everything she'd read about rodents began to play out in a scary, bizarre dream. *She was lying on a tile floor of a laboratory, tickling Surfer. Surfer had collected some interesting things for his nest. A coin. A book. A clock. A fireman suddenly opened the door of the lab and began screaming at Surfer. The fireman was terrified of him, and Surfer began to run away. "Don't go," Sarah called after him. She was able to follow him because Surfer left a trail of secretions on the floor.*

There was a dog in the dream, too. A dog and a cat were trying to eat Surfer, and some nurse came running from out of nowhere and started throwing dry-cleaning fluid on him. "This is for you, Surfer," the nurse kept saying. She tried to touch him with electrical wires, and then she tried to throw him into a clothes drier. "You're a bad rat," the nurse said. "A subway train is going to get you. A special subway to vacuum you up. A vacuum train that will suck up rats while cleaning the tracks. Are you ready to be sucked up? Are you?"

Silence.

It was too silent.

It was the quiet that woke Sarah up. And the darkness. She knew there was a full moon. She'd seen it in the sky the night before—but her room was dark. Too dark and silent. Like snow had fallen. A snow blanket on the house.

But it wasn't winter.

There came a voice.

Muted.

Someone speaking—far away. Or whispering. The sounds were coming from the room where Michael was sleeping. By now, he *should* have been sleeping. Perhaps the sounds were a radio. A DJ talking on a radio. Michael could be listening, frightened. Nightmares. There was no flickering of lights beneath the door. No TV light or streetlight or anything. There was only darkness filling the house.

Sarah got up from the bed. She slipped into her jeans, threw on a denim shirt, and walked barefoot out into the hallway. Aunt B's room was to the right. She'd left on a night-light, a small plastic disc glowing in a wall socket like a Cyclops's eye. The voice was coming from Michael's room, she was certain now.

As she opened the door, she saw his bed was empty—the comforter thrown back. The hair on the back of her neck bristled. Michael was standing in front of Surfer's cage. He didn't seem to know she was in the room.

Sleepwalking, Sarah thought.

Perhaps Michael was sleepwalking like she used to when she was ten or eleven. And she had invented two imaginary friends: Gina and Bono. She'd talk to them when she did her sleepwalking. For a while, even awake, she'd talk to the make-believe Gina and Bono.

"Gina wants me to play Blind Man's Bluff," she'd say. Or "Bono wants me to hot-dog with him in Albuquerque."

And then one day—after about a year—her imaginary friends had stopped coming. About the time her father had bought Surfer for her.

Surfer.

Surfer saw her now. He was up on his haunches—in the faint and ghastly spill of the night—light—staring at her.

"What are you doing?" Sarah asked Michael.

Michael turned to her. He looked frightened as he pointed toward the window drapes.

There was the silence again. The silence of snow. The impossibility of a house nearly dark with blackness while a full moon was in a crystal-clear sky.

Sarah reached out her hand to the wall and flicked on the light switch. The ceiling light burst white and hot like a sun. She felt her mouth was dry and her stomach hurt. She heard the pulse in her temples and her eyes burned as she yanked back the drapes. She stared at the shining window, a vast sheet of thermal glass. Aunt B had used her husband's insurance money to remodel the house with windows that deserved to look out on the river. The vista of the Kull. Windows that should have the light of the moon and the glow of Staten Island homes and rows of Richmond Terrace street-lights from across the water.

But there was another, more liquid darkness.

Behind the glass of the window was motion.

Murky, undulating shapes.

God, what am I seeing? Sarah thought. What is the cloak of hair and brown and wetness on the window? A moment later, the shapes of the indi-vidual bodies became recognizable, like emerging figures in an abstract painting or an inkblot. What she saw before her was slick and oily brown, with patches of lightness. The shroud of hundreds of dark little heads craning toward her from a woven maze of feet and claws. Then she saw clearly the small ugly bodies, bodies streaking the glass like moist, muscular worms.

Rats.

The house was wrapped with rats.

Sarah fought to breathe.

"I think they've come for Surfer," Michael said.

"They want Surfer."

A larger, grisly rat's head suddenly appeared at the left side of the ghastly scene at the window. Crusts of plaster fell into the room. Soon the rat's head was *through* the frame, through the molding and screen tracks and trim. Then another outsized head and claws burst through the frame at the top. Red-rimmed eyes stared from snouted spheres the size of brown cantaloupes. The rats had mangled and undermined the whole of the window support. Their unholy jaws were open, dripping—and their forelegs thrashed—then hammered!—at the glass. The entire window came falling forward.

CRASH.

Sarah grabbed Michael's hand as the window exploded at their feet and the rats raced toward them.

10 • WAR

The two giant rats shrieked into the room on the crest of the clawing wave of smaller rats. Instinctively, Sarah pushed over the TV and its stand so that it thundered down between them and the invading rodents. She heard her aunt's voice. She was in the room, shouting. Aunt B was screaming at the rats and pulling Sarah and Michael away from the snorting, sickening flood.

The largest rats made straight for the bedstead with Surfer's cage.

"No!" Michael cried.

But Sarah and Aunt B held on to him. The cage was on the floor now, and the big rats easily split it open with their savage teeth and claws. Surfer, his whiteness shining at the center of the writhing brown, was up on his haunches, screeching. The room filled with the high pitch of rat cries, and suddenly Surfer was out of the cage and flanked by the largest rats. The rodents raced toward the shattered window.

"DON'T GO WITH THEM, SURFER!" Michael yelled. "DON'T GO!"

Sarah froze at the doorway of the room, watching the rats drain back out the window. There were scraping sounds on the roof and at the other windows of the house, as the covering of rats melted and moonlight broke in to fill the rooms.

Michael shook loose.

In a moment he was at the smashed window. Sarah and Aunt B caught up to him, took hold of him firmly. They stood watching the carpet of rats recede across the deserted street, flow like an oil slick and pour off the center pilings into the black water. For a while longer, Surfer's albino coat shone like a beacon beneath the pier lights. His coat appeared as a fading speck at the front wedge of the rats as they swam south in the Kull.

Aunt B was shaking. "What was that?" she gasped. "What's happening?"

Sarah turned Michael to her. "How did you know they were here for Surfer?" she asked him. "Why do the wild rats want him?"

"I don't know," Michael said. "Surfer's been making sounds. He's been restless. Sounds like when I'd hear him talk to the rats at the dump. Didn't you hear him? Don't you think he talks to them? Rats do that. They talk to each other."

"But what are they saying?" Sarah asked.

"Surfer's been acting strange ever since the mound opened," Michael said. "The mound splitting and the boardwalk and the garbage truck. I want him back! I want him back!" Michael wailed.

"I heard him," Sarah said. "And I heard him with the rats that were on the baby. The Hettles' baby. Surfer made those high-pitched sounds to the rats when they were drinking from the baby's lips. Why, Michael? Why?"

Aunt B knelt down beside Michael and put her arms around him. She said softly, "Do you know, Michael?"

"He sounds like he tells them things," Michael said. "He watches television with me, and then he wants to go out. He'd want to go out to the dump, and he'd run with the wild rats. He'd disappear for a while, and then he'd come back. I really think he told them things. He watches the news and nature programs, and it's like he talks to them. But Surfer's my buddy. He's my best pal!"

Sarah realized she was thinking faster than she could speak. She remembered Surfer and the TV remote. She remembered how Michael couldn't turn the switch on for the garbage disposal. The disposal with the rat. "You think the rats are . . . what, Michael? What? The rats are like . . . Surfer's friends?"

"*I'm* his friend," Michael said. "Me. Surfer didn't want to go with them. I know he didn't." He burst into tears.

Sarah ran her hands through her brother's near-white hair with its dark, dark roots. She moved her hand gently—she wanted him to know she loved him no matter what. No matter what he said or thought or dreamed, no matter how crazy or mad or idiotic any of it seemed. She wanted him to know she wouldn't think the mean things the other kids yelled at him. Stupid Mike. Or Crybaby.

"Does Surfer protect you and me? Is that why the rats didn't attack us at the dump? Why they didn't attack us now? Because of his shrieks. His . . . his *talking* to them?"

"I don't know," Michael said through tears.

Sarah knew what she had to do.

"Aunt B, take care of Michael—and get Dad on the phone!" Sarah shouted as she turned and ran to her room. "I've got to talk to him!"

Sarah switched on the laptop. Now she knew exactly which files her father would have to have. *Rats. Rats can count to the number 43. Their heightened senses. Rats using clotheslines and telephone lines as high wires. Rats in mazes and rat memory, and rats who gnaw off their own legs if they're caught in a trap. Rats who pick other rats to act as tasters to see if bait is poisoned. King rats.*

Emperor rats.

Rats who rule kingdoms of rats. The intelligence of rats. Rats that are smart . . .

Aunt B was in the doorway.

"The numbers he gave me are busy. He's got to be swamped."

Sarah closed the laptop and put on a sweater. "He's going to need this, okay? Janice's computer. I've got more about rats on here than any museum or anybody he's going to find."

"I'll drive us over the bridge," Aunt B said.

"No," Sarah said. "You take care of Michael, and keep trying Dad on the phone. I'll take your inboard. It's twice as fast as the AquaSkiff. I can make it across the river to Stapleton in ten minutes. What pier is he at?"

"Six."

"You're sure?"

"I don't think you should go out on the river," Aunt B said.

Sarah was already heading down the stairs.

Michael came out of his room rubbing his eyes. "I'll go with you," he said. "Surfer's out there. He's out in the river somewhere."

"No, Michael. You stay with Aunt B," Sarah said. "If you get Dad, tell him I'm on my way. Tell him the rats are smart. Tell him I think they know exactly what they're doing. Tell him they were here. Tell him they've got some kind of a *plan*."

"Don't run over Surfer," Michael cried. "I want him to come back. Don't hit him with the prop on the boat. Please don't. Bring Surfer back, please . . ."

Sarah ran out the front door and across the street to the pier. The polished mahogany hull of the watercraft shone beneath the pier lights as she threw off its cover and mooring lines. She slid into the bucket seat behind the steering wheel, turned on the Magneto, and the motor coughed to life.

By eleven P.M., Captain Nagavathy had the forty-ton-steel-hull *Parsifal* cruising through the Narrows and under the Verrazano Bridge. It had been decided that he'd take the route through lower New York Bay, tracing the Staten Island shoreline into the Kill Van Kull and eventually reach the Arthur Kill—where the reports said the main swarm of rats had last been seen. The single Coast Guard cutter out of Fort Wadsworth sailed the opposite way around the island, clockwise, following the south perimeter of the island on the chance the rats had turned toward the Jersey beaches and the open ocean beyond Sandy Hook.

Captain Nagavathy stayed at the helm of the tuna boat while his first mate, Radman, a buffalo of a man in a stained pair of overalls, kept binoculars trained on the murky waters ahead. There were several oil tankers anchored just beyond the Tompkinsville piers, and one of the bright orange Staten Island ferryboats crossed the *Parsifal*'s path off the St. George commuter terminal. From there it was a short sail to the entrance of the Kill Van Kull and the narrows of Bayonne.

"There they are," Radman called. "Ten o'clock portside—off Mariner's Harbor."

"Take the helm," Captain Nagavathy ordered another of the crew. He saw the rippling water a few hundred yards before the abandoned Brewer's dry docks and the ruins of the Richmond Creek overpass. Great slabs of blackened roof were all that were left of the docks, once a major ship repair center and one of the only facilities in the 1940s that was large enough to work on aircraft carriers like the *Intrepid* and *Indianapolis*.

"See 'em?" Radman asked.

Captain Nagavathy glanced at the depth finder and fish locator. He saw his own hands begin to shake as he was filled with a mixture of relief and celebration when he realized how few rats there were. Rats had always made him uncomfortable. He hadn't looked forward to bringing them aboard. He didn't know what would happen, how they would behave. There was a chance the netting wouldn't even work with rats, unless their bodies bent and doubled one on top of the other. It might have been too crude, the webbing too sparse, but maybe the drag through the water could crush them. The flow would mash and press and wedge their bodies together long enough to get them into the teeth of the grinders.

It looked like less than a few hundred square feet of small, swimming rodents, their backs glistening on the surface, splashing, almost like they were waiting to be caught.

It would be over quickly.

Fifteen minutes of garnering work for the *Parsifal*, and the rats would be hauled aboard and ground and drained and packaged. Sure, it'd take a full day to clean out the blood and bone fragments—to flush the equipment and canning machinery halfway clean for a tuna run—but the *Parsifal*'s mortgage would be paid this month. It'd be paid, and Nagavathy knew he'd have a chance.

He'd have a breather from wondering where the next buck was coming from. There'd be time to get up to the Cape and the Vineyard. Time to luck into a school of bluefin or albacore.

Or stripers.

Or cod.

"Drop the nets," the captain yelled.

The two other mates threw the console switches for the automation to begin. There was a metered, controlled release of the shiny steel netting. The men watched the unraveling and listened to the clanking and slipping and scraping. They stood ready to adjust the conveyor guides as the main netting flowed out from the burnished ramps of the stern platform.

Radman took over the helm. He eased the *Parsifal* into a stalking arc. Radman was the best when it came to net positioning, to understanding eddies and wave direction and drift. He commanded top dollar in commercial fishing from a decade of supervising crews on major boats and trawlers from Mexico to the North Sea. A school of wet and exhausted dump rats was going to be easy.

Nagavathy moved to the railing as the boat passed starboard of the school. The dark wiggling bodies looked like mutant fish, like a propagation of porgies or Sargasso eels heading up the mouth of the Hudson. When the net connected with the swarm, the *Parsifal* slowed. The catch of rats started to surface on the aluminum feed ramp. That was when all similarity to a fish crop ended.

There was wailing.

Shrieking.

High-pitched, pathetic sounds as the net pulled the rats up onto the boat. The rats legs and arms were tangled, rat smashed against rat in the net, as they were yanked from the Kull. The operation moved into high gear, and the sounds quieted. The rat sounds began to mute and transform into a whimpering. The sounds became the death gurgles of drowning and suffocation, and the rats gasped. They were rendered into helpless packets of life. Units. Docile meat units being brought aboard.

Suddenly, when the grinding machinery started, the rats became alive and savage again.

"Gaff them," Captain Nagavathy shouted to the mates. "Keep them all on the conveyor."

The men easily hooked and stabbed the errant rats that had managed to leap free of the net. Some were piggybacking onto other rats, and jumping off the aluminum ramp and racing across the deck.

The men laughed at first.

It was like a game.

Like working in a candy factory or a cookie plant. Little dark animals that had to be corralled and knocked and swatted so they'd drop into the gaping hole of the machinery and into the teeth of the whirling chopper blades.

There was a spray of blood and fluids as the first of the rodents were pulverized. Their fleshy pulp and juices dripped into the stamping, howling extruder of the cannery.

"Great," Captain Nagavathy called out to his crew. "Great!"

11 • WAITING . . .

Sarah kept her hand on the throttle as she crossed the Kull waters from Bayonne. There was heavy oil tanker and cargo shipping traffic, and the tide flow was severe. More violent than she'd ever seen it. She was grateful for the moonlight. The full moon. But by now, she had begun to believe that even it was part of some plan.

Smart rats.

Rats as smart.

It made her mind spin, and all the possibilities of what could be happening moved in her stomach like a chilling, pointed claw. Full moon tides always moved the water swiftly through the Kull and into New York Bay. She had gone with her parents on enough late night clam digs and crabbing expeditions to have felt the power of the tide.

Tonight, the water rose higher. Rushed like a true river. What if the rats had known even this? What if they'd deliberately picked this night of all others to break out of the asphalt mounds? What if they knew the only way they could have a chance to find a new home would be on the full moon tide? The fastest drift. The greatest distance. Rats in the river on the night they could travel the fastest and the farthest.

She put on the ship-to-shore of the watercraft. The broadcast belt had been out of commission for years, but she listened to the Coast Guard frequency. Through heavy static, she heard the ship's communications officer talking with the Fort Wadsworth base. The S.S. *Gold Star* cutter was far away—on the other side of the island—past Great Kills and heading for Tottenville and the south entrance to the Arthur Kill.

"They didn't go that way," Sarah said aloud, almost angrily. Couldn't anyone see? Couldn't they have flown out with a helicopter? They would have seen the rats weren't heading south. They were heading for New York Bay! She wanted to shout it into the mike, but she knew no one could hear. Aunt Betty should have had the radio fixed. Aunt B, I told you to do it. I told you.

The radio began to pick up police calls and other floating signals. A patrol car was heading north on Richmond Terrace, trailing a drunk driver. A private ambulance driver was chatting with St. Vincent's hospital. *Slow tonight. I'm stoppin' at the Victory Diner for a burger and fries. Ya want somethin'?*

Sarah kept tuning. She finally found the Coast Guard frequency—and her father's voice! He was on the radio of a second Coast Guard cruiser heading across the bay! He was talking to an officer on the first cutter.

There was static.

More static.

From what she could hear, she figured her father was picked up from the command post and on a cutter somewhere between Ellis Island and the Brooklyn Navy Yard. "There's a small colony of the rats on the Liberty Park beach," she heard her father reporting. "And another, maybe twenty or thirty on the south side of the Liberty Island rock base."

There was a full minute of severe static before Sarah could understand any more of the transmission. "The tide's carrying the rodents fast," the officer from the first cruiser said.

"A zoologist's guess is that they're scouting. . . . Searching . . . they know they've got to move," came her father's voice again. "That's what they do, he said—reconnoiter for the main colony."

"Reconnoiter for what?"

"For food."

Good, Sarah thought. Dad's on to the rats. She

could tell from his voice he knew there was method to the exodus. Design. He knew rats were smart. He had always told her—pointed out—what they were up to at the dump.

Hoarding.

Marking territory.

Scheming.

She considered turning the watercraft about and heading toward the Bayonne side of the Kull. From there she could probably open up the motor to make thirty or thirty-five knots. The run along the Navy docks was usually clear this late at night, and the ferry paths were all closer to Brooklyn and the Verrazano bridge.

She could catch up with the Coast Guard cruiser and signal them. Her father would recognize the watercraft, and they'd stop and she'd pass over the laptop with its data. She played out the scene in her mind. His surprise when he'd see her. He'd probably be ticked off at first—worried about her—but when she explained everything to him, he'd understand. He'd be proud of her, like she was of him. To her, he was no ordinary man. He was Ulysses and a brave adventurer.

And now he'd begin to understand she was a chip off the old block and be very, very proud of her.

Sarah was off the Mariner's Harbor shoreline when she saw the sleek tuna boat cruising slowly off of the shell of the old Brewer's dry dock. The overhang was cantilevered from a four-story network of steel beams. She saw the white water at the surface behind the boat, and the glint of the steel nets being cranked up the stub of the stern. They had hooked into the rats. Rats being taken aboard. She knew she had to warn them.

That there were too many rats. Smart rats. *Billions* of rats.

Too smart to go gently into the night or the boat or anything. Too clever to splash around waiting to be caught. They'd be up to something. They'd have a stratagem.

She goosed the throttle and the watercraft hurtled toward the *Parsifal*. Closer, she cut the speed. A line of long black oil and high octane gasoline tankers were passing into the Gulf Port deep channel. Closer, she saw the mob of rats tangled, pressed together in writhing clumps as they were pulled up onto the trawler's conveyor belt. Captain Nagavathy saw the inboard coming along side. He was surprised to see a young girl at the wheel, and strained to hear what she was shouting to him.

"I'm Macafee's daughter," Sarah yelled.

He finally understood her. Macafee. The guy he'd been talking to. The man from the dump that the Coast Guard had aboard. He began to catch what she was saying. Some kind of a warning. There would be more rats. *More.*

"This is all," he called back to Sarah. "A few thousand."

"I was at the mound when it split open," Sarah yelled. "I was at the dump. There are billions! I saw billions! They're smart," Sarah insisted. "They're very smart."

She saw the captain's attention drawn to a new wedge of rats swimming out from the shore. It looked like only another hundred or two.

"You should get out of here," Sarah called up to him. "You don't understand."

Sarah felt the coldness of fear rise up through her chest. Her throat hurt from calling out into the night air. Maybe she was way off base. Maybe it was her personal terror of death, and she was projecting everything onto the rats. Maybe rats hadn't covered Aunt B's house. Perhaps there was no plan. She knew she sounded crazy. Maybe it *was* all some sort of nightmare or hallucination.

But she knew in her heart that it wasn't.

She threw the inboard into reverse and moved

slowly away from the *Parsifal*. She thought she'd better butt out, and just get the laptop to her father. There would be someone on the Coast Guard cutter who could sift through the files on rats. Someone could bring them up and read them and tell her father everything.

He'd know what needed to be done to stop the rats. Whatever they were up to.

There was something curious about the new wedge of swimming rats as it reached the *Parsifal*. They circled away from the closing, deadly netting. They swam in closer to the stern, avoiding the spin of the huge, lethal blades of the propeller. Sarah watched as the wedge of rats seemed to be searching.

Examining.

Inspecting.

Suddenly, they dived beneath the stern.

Nagavathy was hanging over the railing of the boat trying to keep his eye on the newcomers. By the time he realized what the rats were doing, it was too late. "THEY'RE JAMMING THE RUDDER!" Captain Nagavathy yelled. "THEY'RE JAMMING IT!"

Sarah saw the mate at the helm beginning to struggle with the wheel.

Can't turn it.

Can't turn.

The mates at the conveyor heard the engines shutting down, but not before the *Parsifal* was caught in the tide's shore drift and eddies. The momentum was steady, unalterable—the huge metal boat drifting helplessly between the rotted pilings and under the vast overhang of the abandoned dry dock. Sarah watched helplessly as the current took the tuna boat under the towering roof.

The mates at the stern conveyors began to shout: "The nets have stopped. We can't crank the nets!"

Nagavathy ran to the stern to help. He said, "We're slowing. Everything's fine."

The boat eased beneath the roofing and glazed a string of docking tires on what was left of the swaying pilings and feeble seawall. Nagavathy thought the worst that could happen would be that they'd run aground in the thick floor of grease and mud and bottom debris. They'd only have to hire a tug to ease them out. He'd get the Coast Guard to pick up the tab for that maneuver as well.

"They're coming in the boat," one of the mates at the harvesting belt shouted. "The rats!"

Sarah brought the inboard within fifty feet of the *Parsifal*. With the net dragging in the bank silt, several dozen of the rats rallied to leap off the conveyor and onto the deck. The mates chased them, were swift to kabob them with their pointed and sharp gaffs. They hurled the still-squirming rodent bodies into the processor and the whir of its chopper. All danger seemed past, and Nagavathy was able to laugh.

One of the mates wore an eye patch and a white embroidered shirt. He had a Grateful Dead cap on, with its brim covering old burn scars from a boiler accident. Sarah couldn't help notice him as he lifted his gaze upward. For a moment, he appeared paralyzed, staring up at the dry dock roof above.

He shrieked.

"EEEEHHHHHHH."

Nagavathy and the rest of the crew followed the mate's gaze upward. There was another sound now. High-pitched. Harrowing. The vast ceiling of the molding dry dock was covered with thousands of writhing, small brown and hairy bodies. Rats were hanging, crawling upside down on the rotted roofing, screaming like bats and vultures from hell.

Radman was silent, knowing, reaching quickly for a club. Somewhere—it seemed in his mind—

Nagavathy heard a sound like a deep, pervading death rattle. A strange calmness flooded his whole being, and his eyes drifted helplessly to Radman.

The other mates grabbed gaffs, knives. Sarah understood what was happening. She wanted to shout for them to jump overboard, but another, wider and thick wave of rats had somehow moved in to surround the boat. Their tight, glistening backs lay waiting at the surface like a carpet of horror.

Waiting . . .

The dark, hairy bodies on the ceiling began to drop. Rodents fell like screaming dark lumps of primordial, small, and ghastly brutes. One of the largest rats fell onto the face of the oldest mate. His face had been calm, as if comprehending the inevitable. The rat began biting the man's ear, tearing at it, digging in violently toward the brain. Ellis, the youngest mate, ran from the stern toward an open cabin door. He was insane with fright, shouting.

Screaming.

A half-dozen rats fell onto his shoulders, and began to leap for his eyes. The young mate fell to the deck.

Sarah cried out when she saw the captain fall against a railing. Rats had covered him like an awesome, thrashing quilt. A mass of others raced up

Nagavathy's legs and were beginning to gut him. Radman and another mate rushed to club and stab as many of the rats as they could. Their hands rose up into the air as the rats began to rain down now— a cloudburst of snarling, grease-backed rodents, chewing at Radman's fingers and wrists and eyes.

Quickly, it was Radman alone over Nagavathy's body, as another of the giant rats dropped from above. It fell with its claws extended, digging vehemently into Radman's neck and paralyzing him. Several dozen more of the rats were airborne as the last of the mates tried to throw himself overboard. But the mate's mouth was open in a scream as he tripped. Several dozen rats began to drag him along the deck by his hair and the skin of his back. Another rush of rats were biting the mate's lips, ripping off his cheeks and nose and ears until there was nothing left of his face but a sickening bleeding pulp.

Radman, the last one alive, staggered toward the bow. He broke a glass panel and grasped a fire ax. He managed to lift it into the air, as a final cloud of rodents dropped onto his head. The rats were screeching.

Louder.

Deafeningly.

They plunged their claws like talons into Radman's neck. He threw them off, but as he staggered backward, Sarah could see the gaping scarlet hole where his throat had been. He was dead before his head hit the cold, wet steel of the deck.

"I want to go after Surfer," Michael said, holding the bent and violated rat cage on his lap. He sat solemnly in the living room with the big TV tuned to the local news. The cage's wire exercise wheel was too warped to turn. "He's going to die. They're going to hurt him and kill him and eat him. They took him to do horrible things to him."

"They didn't take him," Aunt B said, fixing the convertible couch with a clean bed pillow and sheets. "He went with them. They tore his cage open, but he went with them on his own."

"No," Michael insisted. "They made him go. I've got to help him. He's my friend and my pal and . . ."

"I'm sorry . . ."

"I want to go."

"You can't," Aunt B said. She was still out of breath from carrying up a pair of scratched and warped plywood closet doors from the cellar and securing them against the frame of the shattered window of her son's old room. "Maybe Surfer will come back," she said. She thought a moment, then groaned. "For that matter, maybe *all* the rats will come back."

Michael held a few of Surfer's food pellets in the palm of his hand. "No—they won't come back," he said. "They're taking him to the dump. I saw where they were heading. They were swimming back up toward the Kill. They're taking Surfer back to the mounds."

"What would they go back there for?"

"Something's still there."

"What?"

Aunt B moved to the bay window and looked out. There'd be no horde of rats coming across the road without her knowing it this time. "To get back to the dump, they'd have to swim against the tide."

"They'll hug the shore," Michael said, remembering about the backflow and eddies of the high tides whenever his father had let him drive the skiff. His dad had taught him the secret of motoring back against a strong current. Close to the shore. Look for the cat's-paws. Catch the whirlpools and backflow.

"Would you like an orange freeze?" Aunt B asked, deciding they both needed something to cheer them up. She headed for the kitchen. "Or cocoa? I'll get us some pretzels. Do you like onion and sour cream potato chips?"

"What's a freeze?"

Aunt B laughed. "I put the juice in a blender with some of the pulp and ice cubes. You'll like it."

"Okay."

Aunt B put on the tiny kitchen TV, got the bag of oranges out from the refrigerator, and started to slice them for the juicer. She used the wall phone to dial Sarah. She had hated cell phones from the moment they had started showing up all over the place, but now she felt a sense of relief when she heard the signal go through—that it was ringing.

"Hello." She heard Sarah's voice. It sounded like she was in an echo chamber, and the static was heavy.

"Sarah, are you all right?" Aunt B asked.

"Yes."

"Where are you?"

"On the river, Aunt B," came Sarah's voice again. Aunt B could hear something was wrong. Very wrong.

"What's the matter?"

"The men . . ." Sarah began to cry. "The men

were attacked. Ambushed. The rats trapped them . . . the men on the tuna boat. It was horrible, Aunt B. They did horrible things to them."

Aunt B felt a vise of fear grip her chest. "Sarah, get back here immediately. I want you back here. Michael needs you. He doesn't look right. He's saying strange things . . . he wants to——"

There was a sound.

The sound of a motor. For a moment, Aunt B thought she might have accidentally turned on the blender. It didn't make any sense, but that was the way so many things were now that she was older. She jumped at sounds in her head. She saw phantom images that flickered on her retinas. Peripheral distortions, one doctor had called it. She'd realized lately that her own brain wasn't a thing to be trusted. But she was certain Sarah was crying now. Something appalling had happened.

Sarah would have to come home.

"Aunt B?" came Sarah's voice. "Aunt B?"

It had taken Aunt B a moment longer to realize exactly what the whirring sound was. The noise that was not in the kitchen. Not even in the house. She dropped the phone and was at the window now. She saw the skiff. The motor she'd heard was the roar of the outboard. Someone was in the Macafees' boat. The boat was moving. Michael was behind the wheel racing north and away from the pier. Her ten-year-old nephew was in the boat and heading for the Kill.

12 • SEARCHING

"How could it happen?" Macafee found himself screaming when the report on the *Parsifal* came in. *"How?"* He knew Captain Ragan of the Coast Guard cutter was staring at him. Oh, yes, I'm a guest on a military ship, he thought. I'm with lieutenants and midshipmen and officers—sailors all. No emotion. Everything by the book. So he suppressed the shriek, drove it deep under his skin and into his stomach. His whole abdomen was pained with confusion and alarm and anger.

The radio engineer kept a line open to his main command tent on Pier Six in Stapleton. With the mayor airborne in a helicopter, there was going to be no more flack from the Staten Island borough president. Macafee's second in command had radioed: "We've got enough generators, telephone lines, and computers delivered here to launch World War Three."

The cutter was off Ellis Island and the Statue of Liberty. Manhattan, with its twin towers and Woolworth building—its cluster of skyscrapers on

Wall Street, and Greenwich Village, and Broadway—it was all there to the north. Towers ablaze with lights at night. Jets roaring overhead to land at LaGuardia. More money and penthouses and Fifth Avenue. And what was everyone looking for? Macafee thought.

Rats!

The Coast Guard was looking for rats, with the mayor on the radio-phone. Macafee was grateful Sarah and Michael were at his sister's house in Bayonne, safe from the madness and the unimaginable horror. The mayor was butting into the whole operation, jockeying for publicity and photo opportunities. The mayor doing good works. The mayor working late for his constituents. The mayor saving New York City again. "I was talking with the Secretary of Health. He says we've got to burn 'em," the mayor said on the phone.

"The rats are gone from the dump," Macafee reminded him.

"You don't know that," the mayor said. "The secretary's been on the phone with India and Malaysia and South America. He knows about rats spawning."

"They're not spawning."

"Swarming," the mayor said. "Whatever they're doing. They said you don't seal over a dump with asphalt. You don't do it. It makes the rats very angry and they have to move. I don't know who the cretins are on your island that did this. What dopes . . ."

"You signed the permits," Macafee said.

"Well, you just listen to me!" the mayor roared. "Those rats are looking for another home, you understand? They're looking, and they're tired and they're desperate. All I'm saying, Macafee, is they'd better not end up in our city's subway tunnels. All we need is a few billion killer rats underneath Manhattan. Do you understand what I'm saying? And they don't move all at once. For your information, rats don't move all at once!"

Macafee was too furious to continue. He passed the phone to John Medina, but switched the call onto the speaker.

"Medina here, Mr. Mayor," John said.

"Who are *you*?"

"Mr. Macafee's assistant."

"Well, you tell him what they told us from Malaysia."

"What, sir?"

"Whenever there's a colony this big, there's always a king. A fat palooka guy that rules all the others. An emperor, with servants and warriors and a massive harem. That's what they call the top dog rodent in Malaysia. The emperor. He calls the shots for the whole colony. He's bigger. Teeth like razors. The swarm finds the new home before he moves. They find it and then they move the emperor. That's what our rats will do as soon as they settle. Move the emperor from the dump. You got that?"

"Yes, sir."

"Oh, yeah," the mayor said. "And tell Macafee that we've decided to firebomb."

Macafee grabbed the phone. "You've decided *what*?"

"You heard me," the mayor said. "The National Guard wants another hour to finish the evacuation. Travis and New Springville are already out. The Army's got six helicopters up at Stewart, and they're being loaded. The best spot burners they've got. They're going in at one A.M."

"I don't think you need firebombs," Macafee said.

"I didn't ask what you thought," the mayor said.

"We're taking care of the emperor and the dump. You find the rest of the rats, and you stop them. You understand?"

"I understand," Macafee said.

"You stop them."

• • •

Sarah felt the tides begin to shift in a kind of seamless elegance as she was torn and anguished about what to do. She knew her aunt would get word about Michael to their father. She'd tell him that Michael had taken the outboard to follow Surfer— that he was heading back toward their house and the dump. She'd make certain they knew about the tuna boat. The terrible deaths of the men. But she couldn't be certain. Not totally.

Aunt B might have trouble getting through. Perhaps she'd try to drive, to go to the police or the Coast Guard base at South Ferry. The Navy Yard. Someplace. Front Street always flooded during a moon tide.

Sarah was overwhelmed. Tears burst from her eyes, and she had trouble getting her breath. An hour before, she had thought everything was set. Secure. Protected. That Michael was safe in Bayonne. She would try to call her father herself. Call the authorities. If the ship-to-shore was working, she could have easily called the cutter. She'd get to her father and the Coast Guard, and they'd help. They'd move quickly. Helicopters. The National Guard. Army and Navy men would be on the spot. They'd find Michael, and he'd be okay.

Alive.

She pressed the "8" button on her cellular phone, the automatic dial for Aunt B's number. There was a loud electronic squawking, and NO SERVICE lit up on the digital face. Sarah realized she'd drifted out of range. The cell phone was undependable around water. Sometimes the signals reflected and bounced to dead or foreign relay towers. She knew what she had to do. *I'm sorry, Michael. Forgive me for leaving you alone. I should have stayed with you at Aunt B's, but I'm coming, Michael.*

I'm coming.

She turned the boat south into the Arthur Kill. Her aunt's boat was faster. She might catch him before he got near the creek that led into the dump. Beyond Mariner's Harbor, she tried the cell phone again, but the signal was devoured and scrambled by the immense span and metal of the Goethals Bridge. She stayed close to the Staten Island shore. In the bright moonlight it was easy to see a small cluster of rats, about a dozen, on the breakwater off Bloomfield. The rats moved in circles, excitedly. Nervously. She saw them go up on their haunches, listen, then drop and shriek to the north.

Like sentinels.

Sentinels.

She had seen the clusters every quarter of a mile or so. They dotted the shore from Travis to West Brighton. Rats, hearing sounds from the south, then turning and shrieking northward. She wondered if the rats were relaying signals. Relaying messages like the cell phone. Like telephone signal boosters.

Rats calling to each other.

Transmitting information.

Rats talking to each other.

"Michael's gone," Aunt B had told her. "He's gone to follow Surfer."

The words haunted Sarah. She turned them over and over in her brain. She thought about opening the laptop cover and turning on the screen. She'd pull up the files, type in RAT SOUNDS. She knew they communicated. That had been part of one of her projects. They spoke in squeals and chatterings: CHIRRRRRR. CHIRRR. And she'd read that they were capable of sounds of such high frequency that humans couldn't here them. She saw jiggles on the boat's sonar screen. Jiggles of sound waving across the glow of the screen.

Rats could talk to each other in someone's house, and no one would even hear them.

She cut the watercraft's speed down as she

turned into Kull Creek. The night wind had picked up again and rushed across her face as she held the boat to the center of the water labyrinth. The cracked mounds stood silent, dead. She could see the vast lifeless fissures where once there had been a cascade of escaping rats. The fractured mound-faces were like cliffs now, the massive chunks of asphalt hanging twisted with great jagged edges. The intricate tiering of compartments and tunneling was all that was left of the rat city. The balconies of dirt and debris were deserted except for shards of rags and bent umbrellas—the tattered flags of garbage that had been exposed to look like exotic altars and deformed faces.

CHIRRRRR. CHIRR. CHIRRR.

With the watercraft idling, she heard the sounds from a small pack of rats on one of the highest tiers. Guards. Spotters.

Sentinels broadcasting in the midst of the desolation.

Sarah knew there would be still more rats below. Rats deep inside the mounds. Special rats, that had been left behind for some reason. She tried to remember what she'd read about the hierarchy of a massive rat colony. What she'd read about king rats and colony invasions and *moving*. Her mind tried to sift through all the data she'd researched for her rat projects. Rat temples and monkey kingdoms and ant colonies and . . .

She thought about opening the laptop, about searching through the files, but she knew her mind was already on overload. She wouldn't be able to think straight. *Where are you, Michael? Where are you?* was all that she screamed in her head.

The wind howled across the shattered mound-faces. The banks were scarred, eroded by the escaping hordes. Whole stretches of the shoreline had been transformed into muddied humps and breaches, covered and mutilated with the tracks and droppings of rats. Any living plants and small trees had been trampled, and steam rose hissing from several of the deepest fissures.

Sarah saw the skiff tied up at the pier of the marina. Michael had docked but he would have to go to their house first before he could find Surfer—if the white rat had returned to the dump. She docked the inboard, leaped out to moor it, and rushed along what was left of the shattered walkway and weblike splintering of the trough. Marge's twisted and contorted truck still lay upside down like a huge extinct lizard, fluids trickling down from its hood and garbage bay.

There were lights burning in the living room of the Macafee house.

Michael! Michael!

There was no sound except for the wind moving through the wind chimes of the porch. She saw the triangulation boxes set up, glowing eerily and unattended, in the middle of the living room. The booster remote lay on the floor beside the coffee table. Michael had set everything up, and the arrows were pointed. Unwavering. Sarah pressed the button on the booster a single time to make certain Surfer's transmitter would be sending at full power. More than two presses might overload the transmitter and give Surfer a shock. She put the booster in the pocket of her jeans. Michael knew where Surfer was, and now so did she.

Sarah opened the pantry cabinet where her father kept all the flashlights and candles, which they used during blackouts from major thunderstorms. The large Coleman lantern was gone, but she grabbed a plain black plastic flashlight and went out through the porch door and onto the back lawn. The arrows had pointed farther south and west than they did on Surfer's usual outings. Triangulating the directions of the needles indicated he was down toward the swamp that interfaced with the largest but flattest of the mounds. Its asphalt lay smooth and intact. Beyond the few ruptured cattails and a narrow tract of skunk cabbages, only the gaping black hole of the huge—thirteen-foot diameter—Willowbrook drainage pipe led into the mound itself.

Sarah placed the strap of the laptop case over her shoulder, and checked to make certain her cell phone was secure on her belt. When she crossed the swamp, she saw the impressions from a boy's sneakers among a vast trail of rat footprints.

"I'll find you, Michael. I'll find you," she vowed as she flicked on the flashlight, waded into the shin-deep water, and started along the horizontal pipe.

13 • HEART OF THE DARKNESS

The water going into the pipe was fresh and clean, part of the small stream from the overflow of Willowbrook Pond several miles to the north. Clean water. Water for rats to drink. Precious water that had fed the colony. She knew Michael had taken the propane lamp, that he had needed it to follow Surfer into the pipe.

The way grew dark and narrow as debris began to appear in the middle of the pipe stream. The pipe itself was made of a thick corrugated tin and iron, but it had rusted and been gnawed at several points, so that tin cans and bottles and broken furniture had fallen in and polluted the water. She felt very alone now. Cramped. Trapped in the pipe. Bad and frightening thoughts gripped her so tightly she could hardly breathe.

"MICHAEL. MICHAEL."

She called again. Her voice reverberated in the pipe, and still there was no answer. Fresh wet footprints of rats were in the silt creeping up the sides of the pipe. At another point where a bureau was blocking the main course of the stream, she saw the marks of Michael's sneakers climbing around, distorted where he had braced against the sides of the pipe, footprints disappearing into the flow of water beyond.

Her clothes were soiled, rumpled, as she switched the laptop and its strap from one side to the other. She felt the booster remote dig into her hip as she walked, and she tried dialing the cell phone again. NO SIGNAL flashed and reflashed. Inside the pipe, she was completely out of contact with everyone.

Michael. Where are you, Michael? Michael?

She jumped at the sight of motion farther up the pipe, at the fringe of the beam from the flashlight. Small rats. Perhaps even mice. Or baby rats just getting out on their own. Babies eating garbage and drinking the water. A hundred feet beyond, the scurrying rodents were clearly rats. They looked like runts. Not large, healthy rats, but ones that might be the servants. Servants and tasters. Small rats that the others dominated and bossed around, like she'd read about in encyclopedias and research books and on the Internet.

In a strange and sad way, the small, frail rats made her think of Michael. Michael. She could hear the bullies after him. *Chicken Mike! Mike, the crybaby rooster head! Here, chick, chick, chick!* For a moment she herself felt all the pain again. The pain of not being liked, of being ridiculed for not being pretty enough or for wearing the wrong clothes or because she lived at the edge of a garbage dump. Of her brother being made to do things he didn't want to. She was sorry she had forgotten all that Surfer meant to him.

Surfer.

Surfer, Michael's friend.

She wanted to call out for her brother again, but something told her not to. She was too deep into the pipe. Too far into the heart of the mound. The bad thoughts began to close around her throat, and her belly became rock hard with fear. Each unexpected gurgle of water or dash of a rat made her nerves fire and her heart jump. Her mouth was scorching, dry, and her eyes began to burn.

The methane, she thought. She would have to be alert, careful of the poisonous and flammable methane. It would be mixed with other gases, she knew. Sulfur dioxide and hydrogen sulfide. And the oxygen she was breathing was a final, explosive ingredient. She knew about the chemistry of the sulfur oxides and dioxides from school, about how they combined with the moisture of an organism's mouth and lungs and turned into acids. Sulfurous and sulfuric acids. Terrible, burning acids.

She felt mush beneath her feet. The silt had become a putrid mud, a sludge of decay and rot and stinking filth. Broken Styrofoam cups and old shoes floated by. She stepped on a license plate, its sharp edge cutting into the side of one of her sneakers.

The flashlight began to dim, imperceptibly—just enough to make the shadows ahead appear to be specters and spirits and ghosts. She could feel time beginning to stand still. There was a sudden flutter above her head. She threw the light beam up onto the ceiling. What she thought was a strip of mold and rust was a blanket of bats.

She felt a scream forming in her throat, but she stifled it. Don't look up. Keep moving. Keep moving and forget about them, forget about the bats.

But her eyes drifted upward again, and she didn't see what was in front of her. Her feet caught, and she fell down into the scum and debris of the water. She dropped her flashlight. It was a glow, a faint glow off to her left in a foot of water, and she crawled toward it, trying to keep the case with the laptop from submerging. She was on her hands and knees, and the thing she tripped on was moving with her, and . . .

It felt like rods and wet rags and it was big. . . .

She grabbed the flashlight and lifted its glow above the surface. There, in the light, she saw what she had dragged—the white curved sticks . . . It took another full second before her mind could understand what she was seeing, and now she was screaming louder than she'd ever screamed before. Her terror echoed and rolled like thunder in the pipe as she tried to push the rib cage away from her. The human ribs and spine with a clump of skin and half-eaten lungs spilling out of it. The skeleton of Hippy, its skull rising above the water with its jaws agape, a morbid laugh beneath the black holes of eyes. A thick black snake shot out of the skull's mouth, as Sarah struggled to get away from the decomposing and mangled corpse.

As though alive, the bones and flesh of the body followed her, followed her screams and terror, and she felt as if her heart would shatter. She pulled and yanked at the legs and disembodied arms, until finally she was free of it and the snake and the sickening stench of rotting flesh.

It was a long while before she could stop her cries and think and control her mind. She saw something. Something that eased her into sanity.

A glow.

At a turn in the pipe.

Michael. It had to be Michael.

Sarah was on her feet again. The water was knee-deep as she reached the light. She saw that the pipe was split, with half of the main branch gnawed and torn away, opening into a shadowy, crude chamber. Michael was beyond the water's edge—at the end of the stall-like space—an area with walls of broken glass and fragments of furniture and rotting news-paper and the soiled stuffing of mattresses. The propane lamp burned in the middle of the ragtag space. Michael was reaching up toward Surfer—Surfer, his albino coat shining atop a mantle of dirt and twisted aluminum tubing where Michael couldn't reach him.

"Michael!" Sarah called, turning off the flashlight and rushing to him. She threw her arms around him, hugged him.

"Thank God, I found you. Are you okay?"

Michael looked at her. He appeared dazed and exhausted. Frightened.

"Surfer won't come to me," he said.

Sarah studied Surfer. She thought she knew his every ritual, his straightforward and predictable rodent behavior. His tiny red eyes stared back at her with a treacherousness she'd never seen in him before. She remembered how easily he'd gone with the wild rats.

"I don't think he wants to be with us," Sarah said gently. "It might be better if we left him alone." Sarah saw motion in the shadows at the edge of the room. Rats began to move out from the darkness toward them. They looked robust and hardy, the biggest rats she'd ever seen.

"We have to get out of here," Sarah said, trying to take Michael's hand.

"No," Michael said.

"Michael . . ."

"Not without Surfer."

The rats flowed toward Sarah and Michael like a thick dark liquid and surrounded them. Some were a foot to two feet long, their glistening, segmented tails dragging behind them in the silt. A horde of smaller rats began to fill the entrance to the chamber and block the exit to the drainage pipe.

CHIRRRR.

CHIR. CHIR.

Surfer was making rapid, excited sounds. He was down on the chamber floor now, staying close to the mouth of what looked like a labyrinth of tunnels. Surfer was signaling, chattering. Like he was talking to the wild rats. The rats halted their approach toward Sarah and Michael.

We're not being killed because of Surfer, Sarah thought—Surfer is telling the rats something. Surfer has some sort of *place* in the colony. A ranking in the hierarchy.

For a moment, Sarah considered that Surfer might be the King Rat . . .

For a moment.

There was a sound from the darkest, widest hollow.

Sarah saw the shadow of something. Something bulky—large!—something bigger than any living thing she'd seen at the landfill. Larger even than the muskrats or the possums or the raccoons.

CHIRRR. CHIRR.

She felt her body numb as Surfer ran in next to the shadow.

The sounds that came now were deeper. More guttural. Disturbing—like rumblings from a jungle. There was a troubled breathing.

Something alive.

Wheezing. A large animal that had asthma or water in its lungs or . . .

Sarah looked to the exit, but it was plugged with rats. The largest rats began to close in further on Sarah and Michael. "Surfer may not be our friend anymore," Sarah said.

"Yes, he is," Michael said. "He tells them not to hurt us."

RRRRRRRRING. RRRRRRRING.

Sarah jumped at the sound from her cell phone. She'd forgotten about it. Thought it was useless, far out of range down deep in the mound. The INCOMING CALL readout was lit and pulsing.

RRRRRING.

Answer it, she told herself. Just answer it.

She pulled up the phone's fragile aerial. She felt a breeze and quickly looked up. A honeycomb of tunnels spiraled and twisted upward, and in the center was a shaft that rose straight above them several hundred feet. She saw stars and moonlight and realized how the signal had reached them.

"Sarah," came a familiar voice.

"Aunt B?" Sarah said into the phone.

"Sarah, where are you?" Aunt B's voice was filled with treble and resounding like an echo. "Did you find your brother? Did you?"

"Michael's with me," Sarah whispered. Sarah didn't want the rats to hear her. Not her fear. Not hear it or see it or smell it. "We're in trouble . . . we're down . . . we're deep inside . . ." She had to take a deep breath before she could go on. "The

Willowbrook drainage pipe . . . oh, Aunt B . . . rats . . . there are big rats . . ."

"Are you at the landfill?" Aunt B asked. "The mounds? Are you back there?"

Sarah said, "We're down deep . . . deep in the mounds . . . beneath the mounds."

"Sarah, can you hear me?"

"Yes, Aunt B."

"The signal's breaking up. Sarah, you have to get out of there. They're going to firebomb it. It's on TV. All the channels. Your father—the Army—Sarah, there are jet planes. They're going to bomb it. Firebomb the dump."

"Help us, Aunt B!"

"Get out! Get out of there now!"

"Tell Dad, Aunt B. Call Dad. Tell him we're here."

The phone went dead in Sarah's hand. She jabbed with her finger at the POWER ON switch. The battery was dead. The only sounds now were from the rats. Rats moving in. Closing. Rats pouring between her and Michael.

Rats surrounding them.

Aunt B's hands were shaking as she tried to open the prescription container. The childproof top finally loosened and she swallowed a single beta-blocker capsule. She had felt the pain in her heart from the moment she realized Sarah and Michael were back at the landfill. She had to shut off the television. She couldn't watch the live video of jet fighters with rockets and bomb racks preparing for takeoff from Stewart Airport.

She began to feel confused when she kept pressing the redial button for her brother's cellular phone. She knew he was on one of the Coast Guard cutters. She would shout the words. Shout:

YOUR KIDS. YOUR KIDS ARE AT THE LANDFILL. THEY'RE THERE. STOP THE BOMBING. STOP FIREBOMBS!

When she couldn't get through, she called the police. *We don't understand what you're saying. Miss, we're not authorized to . . . what's your address? Miss, we're asking for your address . . . we don't know about bombs. What jurisdiction are you in? Miss, we'll have a detective call you back . . . that kind of language isn't going to get you anywhere, ma'am . . .*

She would have to take the car, Aunt B told herself. She'd drive to the Coast Guard base near Liberty Park. She'd drive and keep redialing her brother. There might be a policeman on the street. A squad car. She could stop a squad car or someone who'd know what she was talking about. She would stay calm and try to relax, and the pain in her heart would go away. If the planes flew over the landfill they'd see . . .

They'd see the kids and they wouldn't drop the firebombs and . . .

Aunt B got into her old sedan. She was angry she'd left the windows open, but that was the kind of thing she'd been doing lately. The kind of thing the beta-blockers and the aspirin therapy did to her mind. They slowed her heart and thinned her blood so she wouldn't have a stroke or a thrombosis.

She started the engine, backed out of the driveway. She glanced up at the shattered front window and frame of the house, and prayed that it wouldn't rain.

She'd hurry.

She had to go the speed limit. Faster. Perhaps a cop would stop her. He'd pull her over and she'd explain everything and he'd take over. He'd make all the right calls for her and they'd believe him and . . .

Aunt B gave it gas on the straightaway of Swamp Road. She was aware of a strange odor in the car, as if she'd left some sort of hamburger or milk container or piece of fried chicken to rot. She began to go over what she'd say if . . . The thought chilled her . . . if the children died.

If Sarah and Michael were trapped and burned.

I tried. Oh God, I tried to save your children, Mack. I called. I tried the police and the operator and the phone repair line. I tried everyone and I drove. I drove faster than I've ever driven before . . .

She felt strange sitting in the seat. The car seat. It felt as if it were moving. A faint vibration as though there was a child sitting in the backseat, someone with their feet up against the leather of the front seat. She knew she was imagining things, but she glanced in the rearview mirror. What is that, she wondered? There were moving shadows and her seat began to throb. Shake. A moment later, she felt the chill of wet fur crawling across the back of her neck.

14 • FIRE

Sarah trembled as the rats flowed between her and Michael.

"Surfer won't let them hurt us," Michael said.

Sarah moved so her back was against a wall of springs and stuffings and ruptured aluminum cans. The rats washed up onto her now, several of the larger ones moving up onto her chest, weighing her down. Pushing her down. She followed their lead, wanting them to know she was cooperating. She would do what they wanted, and she would wait for the right moment and . . .

They wanted her on the ground.

Flat.

Still.

Sarah felt a click in her mind as she lowered herself. It was as though a switch had been thrown, something that had pushed her beyond terror and made her think clearly. She felt alert. More alert and alive and aware than she'd ever been in her life. Everything was being processed at once. The planes that were coming. Firebombs. Planes that would rain fire down onto the landfill. They might even survive that. She and Michael and the rats. The planes would fire the asphalt. The surface. The bombing probably wouldn't go deep enough. It probably wouldn't go down to the main pockets of methane and oxygen and safety tunnels the rats had dug. The rats would survive like cockroaches in an atomic blast. Cockroaches that survive volcanoes and hurricanes and demolitions.

Cockroaches and rats, which survive anything. Parts of the colony always live.

The guttural sounds began again, with Surfer rushing to the mouth of the largest hollow. Sarah lay still as a massive, murky shape emerged toward the dimming light of the lamp. At first it was a silhouette, a dark shape the size of a mastiff dog with bright, watering green eyes. A chill began to creep back into the base of Sarah's spine as a monstrous rat form dragged itself toward her. God, what is it? she thought. It moved like a lizard, with long hair and a head of barklike skin.

"Don't make a sound," Sarah told Michael. He was frozen at the base of the far wall, rats covering him like a damp, shaggy rug.

The murky shape snorted, and in the full light of the lamp it was clearly a rodent. Three—four feet long. Bigger than a capybara. Bigger than any kind of rat she'd every heard about. The emperor rat, Sarah thought—he's a mutant king, fed and grown in an underworld of waste fowl and suet and filth and gas. The creature's jaws were thicker, more pronounced than the other rats, with the teeth and musculature of a predator. He came closer to Sarah.

Closer.

His hot, stinking breath stung in her nostrils as he neared. The smaller rats nervously made way for their leader to approach. He moved his snout to Sarah's feet, and a hot froth of saliva vomited out of his mouth and onto her legs as it slowly, carefully, sniffed at her.

"If you ask me, the rats are in New York Bay, and heading north," Macafee told the commanding officer. Captain Ragan looked up from a desk in the officer's room on the Coast Guard cutter, and stared at him coldly.

"Our sister cutter has spotted rats retreating in the Kull."

"It could be decoys," Macafee said. "Whatever we think they're doing, it turns out to be something else."

The captain turned his attention back to his notes. "If they're going to go anywhere, it'll be

Newark Bay. It's closer for them. They've got to be hungry. Desperate. A slick of them has been seen in Secaucus. That means the Meadowlands and outlet stores. Probably Giants' Stadium and the racetrack."

"It's almost two o'clock in the morning," Macafee said, trying to keep his temper and sanity. "There's not going to be any food there. A couple of horses in a stable can't be what they need to move a colony like this."

"I've got orders to lay down an oil slick off Newark. When the rats hit it, we'll set it on fire."

Macafee's cell phone rang. His sister was talking too fast. Too disturbed. He caught that there had been rats in her car, that she had almost crashed. And he heard the words, "The kids are at the dump. The kids are there. You've got to stop the planes. The kids are there!"

The blood drained from Macafee's face as he finally understood—finally believed what he was hearing. He was off the phone now, shouting, "OH MY GOD, CALL OFF THE AIRCRAFT. STOP THE FIRE-BOMBS. MY KIDS ARE OUT THERE. THEY'RE AT THE LANDFILL. GET ME THE COLONEL ON THE RADIO. GET HIM. GET ME OFF HERE. GET ME OFF THIS SHIP NOW!!"

● ● ●

The swollen eyes of the emperor rat moved in their wet, grainy sockets. It stared at Sarah as he sniffed at her feet and legs. Sarah glanced up to Surfer, who was chattering softly from his ledge. The monster rat was examining her like she used to examine and exhibit Surfer. Like Surfer at school when he was her experiment.

Surfer squeaking—chirring—as though telling the king rat what to do. *How* to do it.

Now she was their experiment.

The mutant moved up along her body, until his snout was in her hair. *He's gathering information,* Sarah told herself. *He wants to know where I've been, what I've been doing—what I've been touching.*

What I've been . . . eating.

He began to hiss and open his mouth. Sarah felt his tongue on her brow. It was rough, like a cat's. A tongue licking salt from her, checking her . . . rats with sensitive tongues and whiskers and snouts that can feel everything, that can find their way in the dark and . . .

CHIRRRRR. CHIRRR . . .

Surfer still chattering, advising, as the emperor slid his tongue over her closed eyes.

Several miles away, the tide had begun to recede

off a mud bank, and where no one could see them, the leaders of the main rat horde paused and listened. There came the urgent call, the high, delicate shrieking they'd been listening for.

The hungry and loyal horde turned, began dashing decisively to execute the final order. The final solution. The vast wave of fur and pattering feet raced along the dark shoreline. In front of them, across an expanse of New York Bay, was the shining skyline of Manhattan.

The sickening stench of the carnivore filled Sarah's lungs. An *omnivore*, she corrected herself. A thing that would eat anything. When she opened her eyes, the emperor rat's gray flaring nostrils were inches away. The hissing was coarse now, like a cobra's, and his tongue slid out onto her lips. She felt his tongue prying her lips apart, and she began to cry. She wept and shook, but she wouldn't scream. She wouldn't do anything to make it angry.

Nothing to make it kill her or Michael or . . .

His tongue passed between her lips now, checking her teeth. Its roughness flicked up to inspect the roof of her mouth. The rat's snout was against her face, pressing his tongue so it could sense, examine, know everything she had tasted or swallowed or . . .

She began to gag and try to move away, but the king crawled up onto her, pressing her shoulders back with his paws. He wasn't finished with her mouth, and as his tongue slid up her chin toward her lips again, she remembered the laptop.

The laptop.

She moved her hand slowly to the metal catch on its side and unzipped the cover.

The giant rat felt her motion and retracted his tongue. He looked at Sarah curiously, watched her gently slide the black plastic shell of the computer out of the case. She lifted its lid slowly and pressed the oval ON button.

There was an initial chime, and Sarah booted up the Creature Feature game. The king and all the rats—all of the hierarchy stared as the screen lit up and the background music began to play. "You'll like this," Sarah said nicely to the emperor. She spoke to him softly. Sweetly. As if he could understand what she was saying. She saw that the rat looked interested.

All the rats.

Interested in the bright colors of the computer game on the screen. There were twirling red circles and animals dashing through loops. A jungle of neon and Day-Glo crazy images.

CHIRRRR. CHIRRR.

The king's sounds became a purring. A low vibrating sound. The images were mesmerizing the rats. Sarah kept talking. It didn't seem to matter if what she said made sense. She simply spoke kindly and gently through her terror.

Cordially.

Speaking any gentle nonsense that came into her head. "You see, you can learn a lot from this, dear rats. These are beautiful drawings of kangaroos and birds flying, and they can tell you the mystery of how to get food and how to shop and where to go on Saturday nights and . . . Watch closely. You'll see strange candies and evil leprechauns, and some day I'll take you all to the movies and you'll see hot-dogging and learn how to rock 'n' roll and . . ."

Only Surfer chattered nervously.

Telling.

Squealing.

"Come on, Michael," Sarah said softly, as she slid away from the king rat. Slowly, she stood up. Carefully, she lifted the laptop with its glowing screen. In a moment, Michael was on his feet, too. His hand was in his pocket, and before she could stop him, he had taken out Surfer's leash. He snapped it onto Surfer's collar before the rat knew what was happening.

The white rat sounded ticked off as Michael stuffed him into his jacket pocket and snapped it closed. Sarah moved with the computer open, keeping the screen facing the rats. The ones blocking the doorway looked dazed by the light and the moving, bright images.

Sarah moved steadily forward.

The swarm of rats parted, made room for her to pass. When Sarah and Michael were nearly clear and back in the massive dank drainage pipe, the laptop began to make whirling and clicking sounds.

It switched automatically into its power-saving mode.

The images and sounds of the game faded and the screen went dark. The rats began to chatter angrily.

"RUN!" Sarah shouted at Michael, snapping the laptop closed. "RUN!"

Michael sprinted from Sarah's side as she shoved the laptop into its case and flung the strap over her shoulder. They left the Coleman lamp behind, but she turned on the flashlight. She felt the strain of the incline now, the tilt that made the water flow down into the depths of the mound.

"They're going to firebomb," Sarah shouted to Michael. "Planes are going to bomb the dump, unless Aunt B got through. We have to get out."

The sounds behind them now were savage and reverberating. CHIRR. CHIRR. CHIRRRRR. The racket was a pulsing now. Unified cries of a horde coming after them through the pipe. There was splashing and a violent high pitch, rats modulating sounds higher and higher until the volume was earsplitting.

Michael was faster than Sarah. As they neared the end of the huge pipe, they both could smell the fresh air.

Bracing, cool air.

Air with less gas than below.

Air with less methane and other gases that poison and burn. The mix of oxygen and the hydrocarbon gases below had been barely enough to stay alive. It was just enough to breathe and scream and run.

Enough oxygen and methane to . . .

To *ignite*.

Sarah remembered the booster remote in her jeans pocket, and the transmitter around Surfer's neck. The remote and the transmitter—and the sparking that would happen if she pressed the remote more than once. The charge that would spark and fire.

The shrieking of the rats was nearer—closing. Sarah knew the bigger rodents could reach the top, dash out of the pipe and other fissures in the mounds, and overtake them in the swamp. The rats would divide and ambush and kill. There was the sound of something very large coming through the water. Something enormous and blustering behind them.

"Let Surfer go," Sarah told Michael. "Let him go."

"No," Michael said. "He's mine. You gave him to me. He's my friend."

Michael saw the booster remote in Sarah's hand.

He saw it and heard Surfer squealing in his pocket, and he remembered the gas below—and understood what Sarah planned to do. The sounds from behind them in the pipe were chilling. Primordial. The rats were coming, and Michael knew what would happen if . . .

"Please, Michael," Sarah said, gasping for breath. She began to struggle, to find the water rushing against her legs too powerful—crippling. She slipped on the silt. The terrible, angry guttural sound was right behind her now.

Michael stopped near the opening of the pipe. He reached into his pocket, and felt a sudden pain. He pulled out his hand and saw a trickle of blood on his finger.

"Surfer bit me," Michael said as Sarah caught up to him.

"I'm sorry," Sarah said. She saw the hurt and anguish in her brother's eyes, and knew that he at last understood what Surfer had become. Michael let Sarah take the white rat out of his pocket. She set him down and unhooked the leash.

"See you, Surfer," Sarah said.

"Good-bye," Michael said softly, sadly.

Surfer stared at them for a moment—as if trying to understand what they were up to—then ran back toward the shrieking and the gnashing and the subterranean sounds of fury. Michael grasped Sarah's arm, helped hurry her along the last few feet to the end of the pipe. They ran away from the pipe and across the mound.

"I'm sorry, Michael," Sarah said, as she pressed the button on the remote. She pressed it hard a second time, and yet again. She held it until . . .

. . . there came a sound.

A whooshing.

Sarah had read about that sound. The whooshing of fumes igniting. Men cleaning giant gasoline storage tanks in Bull's Head. There had been fumes in the tanks—the survivors spoke of the whooshing sound that meant death.

The sound of flames moving swiftly.

"Come on," Sarah said, running toward the pier. She could see the moored watercraft and the skiff, as a thick blue flame thrust out of the massive drainage pipe.

In the sky, there came the roar of jets. Five or six sleek black silhouettes passing right over them. Jets flying low over the fractured mounds as tongues of blue flames flew out of everywhere now. Fissures glowing from a deep inferno.

The jets were over them again, surveying at only five hundred feet. Sarah saw the firebombs and missiles strapped to the underbellies and spare gasoline storage cylinders on the wing tips. The pilots didn't seem to see Sarah or Michael, as the planes passed lower still. Trial runs, Sarah thought. She'd read about the trial runs before an actual bombing. Even if she and Michael made it to the watercraft—it was the fastest—she knew they wouldn't be out of range in time.

Suddenly, there came a different roar.

It sounded like the bellow of an angry monster. Its huge dark form began to lift above the horizon of a ruptured mound. An Army helicopter that was lit like a spaceship rose and hovered above the pier. Shafts of white light blasted down from floodlights mounted on its sides, and there was a familiar face among the soldiers in its open bay.

"Dad!" Sarah yelled.

Michael called with her, and ran ahead. In a few moments their father and the two crew soldiers had pulled them into the chopper's bay. They were aboard, and the pilot was lifting them away and into the night sky above the Kull. The squadron of missile jets waited for the helicopter to clear and then did a final pass over the landfill, dropping their payload of fire. The first of the surface explosions came and, for a moment, the landfill blazed like a volcano.

"Thank God, you reached us," Sarah said, hugging her dad.

Michael had buried his head in his father's chest and was crying. Finally, the three of them looked out through the chopper's windows. There were several smaller blasts at the surface of the dump. Fireballs rolled across the mounds and spit up from the tunnels below like eruptions from a Roman candle. When the final explosion came, it filled the sky with bright yellow tongues of fire—and the chopper shook.

15 • FINAL ORDEAL

"I t's not over," Sarah heard her father shout over the din of the chopper's rotors.

"I know," she said.

The chopper shifted, and Macafee put one arm tightly around his daughter, the other around his son. They held fast in the rear on hard seats of plastic and woven bamboo—behind the jump seats of the two young soldiers. The pilot banked the helicopter sharply and followed the Kull north. One of the soldiers was on the radio. There was static and loud voices on the speaker.

Then a frantic officer's voice:

"THE RATS ARE ATTACKING. THE RATS ARE ATTACKING!"

There was more static and garbled shouting on the speakers. The radioman switched the signal to his headphones. He turned around to Macafee. "They're attacking people on the Manhattan Sports Pier. They're after people Rollerblading. Bowling. Everything they've got there. The rats have trapped them—there's a dance—some kind of charity—at least a thousand people are trapped out there!"

Michael began to tremble. "Are the rats going to eat more people?"

"I don't know," Sarah said. "*People* eat people, if they get hungry enough."

Her father had leaped up next to the radioman.

There were screams on the speakers now. A man shouting again. Shrieking. "THE RATS ARE CLIMBING OVER EVERYTHING. THEY'RE BITING. OH, GOD . . ." The man's voice was breaking.

Sobbing.

The helicopter roared through the sky over the Jersey Naval Yard. Wall Street and the West Side Highway were a blur. Within minutes, the roof-landing pad of the Manhattan Playland and Sports Pier was dead ahead.

The pier stretched out into the Hudson River, thousands of pilings reaching up from the black water like dark fingers clutching the main pier and its extensions. The beginning of the pier was covered with a flow, like dark lava. Sarah stared down from the chopper window at the lights and vast nets of the golf range. Everything was ablaze with floodlights except for the amusement park annex. Its metal-tube roller coaster, Ferris wheel—all the rides—sat in darkness like the skeleton of a leviathan carcass.

"You wait in the chopper," Macafee shot at Sarah and Michael as the chopper landed. "You keep the motors going," he ordered the pilot as he jumped out with the two soldiers.

"We want to go with you," Sarah said, but he was gone.

She watched him and the soldiers run across the roof to the pier's glass control booth. There were several police waiting for him, guns drawn. They spoke quickly, as the shrill noise of sirens cut through the night. Sarah saw her father checking the TV monitors. A moment later and all the men raced toward a roof door, and disappeared down into the heart of the pier.

"Get away from the bay door," the pilot said nervously.

"Close it before they come in here," Sarah said. "Rats can jump, you know."

"Both you kids just shut up and wait for your father," the pilot said. Michael began to cry again.

Sarah took Michael to the backseat of the chopper and looked out the rear window. Rats were flooding up along the concessions—TATTOO ASYLUM; TORTILLA GRILL; BIKES AND BLADE RENTALS; ANIMAL HOUSE BAGELS

AND CAPPUCCINOS. She could see down into the open air Rollerblade rink. The swarm of rats cut through the Rollerbladers like a ginsu knife as they leaped onto the crowd, some rats clinging to people's skates and then climbing up their legs— other rats were able to jump high enough to grab hold of some skaters by the throat.

Blood formed in pools, growing larger and larger, expanding with every pulse of a vein. Bladers skated for their lives through the pools of scarlet, their skates splashing like the wheels of a speeding car through a puddle.

Losing hold of her mother's grip, one girl screamed as she tried to pry a rat loose from her leg, but as she rolled past a fallen classmate, the wheels of her skates became slippery with blood and she lost her balance—tumbling onto the hard floor and scraping her knees. A pack of the rats raised their snouts to the air, sniffed, then changed direction as foam and spittle dripped from their mouths. Within seconds, they had pounced on the girl's leg and began to tear at it and feed on it like vultures, each fighting the other for a chance to feast on the human tissue.

Sarah saw a flow of rats rushing onto the landing pad.

"Close the door," Sarah yelled at the pilot.

"I told you to shut up."

Sarah grabbed Michael and rushed forward. "You close it now, you nasty idiot. They're here! The rats are here!"

Rats began to leap up into the chopper. The pilot looked terrified as he tried kicking at them. He left the controls and tried stamping on them, but more kept jumping up at him. One sunk its teeth into his arm, and he started to try to scrape it off on the sharp metal frame of the door.

"Take off!" Sarah shouted.

The pilot knew she was right. He started back into his seat, and grabbed for the controls. A dozen more rats had climbed up from the chopper's landing struts, and were at his feet. Another, larger rat had crawled up the back of the pilot seat and began to bite at the side of his face.

Sarah saw the pilot flailing madly, throttling the motors toward takeoff speed. Instinctively, Sarah grabbed Michael and the laptop, and leaped down out of the bay door. She kept her speed, dragging Michael with her along the roof and moving too fast for the rats to take hold. Behind the cockpit glass, she could see the distorted face of the pilot, clawing to pull the rat from his face. Several others were on his neck, but the rotors were committed to takeoff speed. The chopper began to lift.

"Hurry," Sarah screamed at Michael. She half-dragged him along toward the empty control booth. In a second, the chopper was roaring, lifting up into the air. The rats were biting at the pilot's eyes, and the helicopter began to bank, to swerve sharply off the pier and toward the netting of the pier's golf range. In a second it was on its side and falling down . . . down onto a concrete slab. The rotor blades became shrapnel as they hit, slivers of steel flying everywhere. Sarah pulled Michael into the control booth and slammed the door behind them. A moment later, the chopper became a bomb, its fuel tanks exploding and engulfing the cockpit.

"Where's Dad?" Michael said, trembling.

"I don't know," Sarah said. She set the computer down in the corner and sat Michael in one of the black leather seats in front of the main console. There was a wall of TV screens flickering with images of the tracts of the pier. "Don't look," she told him.

She went to the main slab of glass that looked down onto the different cubicles and sports arenas. Whatever she couldn't see there was on the screens.

People were trying to club the rats with their nine-irons and escape from the golf range.

The rats had completely covered the ball retriever's caged cart like bees on a hive. The driver screamed as the rats' hungry eyes glared at him and their teeth gnashed at the steel protective caging, impossible to penetrate—but as balls were sucked into the car, so were the rats. The driver sensed something behind him and turned around in his seat. Several rats leaped on to his shoulders, neck, and head. The rats sunk their powerful jaws into his skin. One bit into his ear and hung like a dark, swollen earring dripping blood. The driver did his best to fight off the rats, but the cart swerved out of control. With its cage nearly filled with the frenzied rodents, the cart crashed through a barrier and plunged thirty feet down with a huge splash. With its screaming driver, it disappeared beneath the murky water of the river.

Sarah's eyes turned to a different monitor, where rats were pouring down the face of the cliff-climbing franchise. A few of the climbers, including a terrified young woman, were dangling from ropes in the air held safely high and away from the floor of rats by a muscled anchorman on the ground. But the rats started climbing up his legs, their claws ripping into his calf, his knee, his thigh . . .

Valiantly, he was able to swat the first few away, but the smell of blood just brought too many. He tried escaping, but nothing could stop the rats that bit at his waist and chest—and then began to gnaw at his fingers. He tried to hold on to the rope keeping the female climber up in the air, but the rope in his hand slipped inch by inch as the rats bit deeper. More violently. Inevitably he began to submit to the rats, letting the rope slide.

Slowly.

Painfully.

Above, the swinging woman's fate was sealed as she plunged into the waiting horde. Her screams filled the air as the rats bit into her and began dragging her toward the edge of the pier.

Sarah spun around as she heard scratching noises on the door of the control booth. She looked up as she heard the pattering of a thousand small feet on the ceiling. Her heart was pounding through her chest as she heard the sound of small animals crawling in the ventilation ducts. She smelled remnants of the dump, the foul garbage smell that filled the air and clung to rat fur with its sickening stench. Her mind was racing, confused, bewildered, as death clustered around the door and window frames of the control room. Horrors filled the TV screens around her.

Please let it be a bad dream! Sarah thought as a lump of terror formed in her throat. She could barely breathe. All she could hear was the sound of her heart pumping as the world started to spin and everything began to turn white. Sarah knew she was about to faint—when something squeezed her trembling hand.

"Where's Daddy?" Michael wanted to know.

Sarah's eyes opened and the whiteness disappeared as she looked down at her brother tugging at her. "I don't know," Sarah said, flicking tears away from her eyes. "I don't know." Her eyes shot to the sea of dials and equipment of the control panel.

Spotting a microphone, she pushed a button on the PA controls. "Dad, can you hear me?" she shouted into the microphone. She could hear her voice coming back to her through the loudspeakers, and she turned up the volume. Her voice began to reverberate.

Echo.

"Dad, we're in the control room. Dad, where are you?"

The monitors on the front of the pier showed several police cars and National Guard vehicles pulling up out front. There were other odd-shaped military vehicles, modified Hummers and trucks with standing metal tanks of compressed gases. She couldn't see her father among the scurrying MPs and soldiers.

"The rats," Michael screamed, pointing to a corner of the ceiling. "The rats are coming in!"

Sarah saw the first claws and teeth biting away at Sheetrock and wood stripping. Michael was holding on to her, as she turned back to stare helplessly at the wall of screens.

On one monitor was the young crowd at a cotillion formal dance. Teenage girls in gowns and boys in tuxedos were fleeing beneath the sparkle of a turning disco ball swarming with rats. The weight became overwhelming and the ball fell, smashing into the middle of the dance floor. The kids screamed as rats started raining from the ceiling like bats dropping from the roof of a cave.

Rats hit the floor and started climbing up onto the kids, biting them, gnawing into their arms, and crawling up the sides of the white gowns. One boy was paralyzed with terror and sat down in the middle of it all, his face blank as a bulge slowly moved under the back of his tuxedo. The dancers tried to run, but the rats were everywhere—screams of pain and fear filling the air as kids started to trample each other. The members of a string orchestra clutched at their instruments, jabbing them defensively as the rats approached.

The screens showed rats after the bowlers and in the restaurants. There was a rat in the middle of an abandoned vat of spaghetti, its slimy dark body wiggling, crawling among the white glistening strands. A mob of the rats had invaded the batting cage concession, and cornered half a dozen people. A father pulled his son closer to him as a large rat approached with pieces of long blond hair dragging from its mouth.

In the control room, Michael had stopped crying. If anything, he suddenly looked very angry. "Can't we stop the rats?" he asked. "Can't we *kill* them?"

Sarah looked at him. It was the first time she'd ever seen him look furious instead of tearful when it seemed like he was going to lose a fight. Rats were clawing their way into the control room—and running down the walls.

"We stopped them before," Michael said.

"Yes, we did," Sarah said softly.

She remembered she still had the computer. She had stopped a pack of rats once. Why couldn't she do it again? She set the laptop up on the console, and opened the screen. She remembered the rats were mesmerized by Creature Feature. The rats were calm, soothed, as long as the images danced on the screen.

Michael had found the remote for cutting back and forth to additional cameras on sports pier.

"There's Dad," he said happily.

Sarah saw their father in a dim, cellarlike room.

A room with electrical boxes and circuits and hanging raw cables. She grabbed the microphone. "DAD, WE CAN SEE YOU ON THE MONITORS." She saw him react—knew he could hear her. "DAD, THE RATS GET HYPNOTIZED BY LIGHTS. LOTS OF COLORED LIGHTS— LIKE LIGHTS ON A COMPUTER GAME. THAT'S HOW WE GOT AWAY AT THE DUMP. GAME LIGHTS TRANSFIX THEM LIKE DEER IN A CAR'S HEADLIGHTS."

She could tell he had heard her, but she understood there was nothing he could do. There would be no computer game large or dazzling enough to stop these rats.

Unless . . .

She brought up the dark area of the pier. She saw the large rolling hills of steel tubing, the gondolas of the dead Ferris wheel, and red and blue banners swinging in the night breeze. "DAD," she continued into the mike, "TURN ON THE AMUSEMENT PARK LIGHTS. TURN THEM ALL ON."

"I think he heard you," Michael said.

They watched their father on the screen talking to one of the pier engineers. They men moved quickly to a series of metal boxes with heavy switches. The engineer reached up and began pulling down a half dozen of the switches.

The control room ignited with color as the amusement park area burst into bright, gaudy light. Huge neon flickered, whole banks of orange and red lights alternated and flashed. It was as if the whole pier was lying at the base of a giant pinball or computer game.

Sarah looked back at the monitors.

The rats were still attacking. She ran to the slabs of glass that were the control room windows. Rats had bitten and overwhelmed half of the skaters, and were dragging more of the bodies over the side of the pier.

"Why aren't the rats stopping?" Michael asked. "Why don't they stop?"

"They want the people in the water," Sarah said through her tears. "Bodies in the water. They'll take them down. Store them. Finally drag them into the tunnels. The city's tunnels."

The first of the rats made it through a molding and dropped into the control room. It fell near them, but knew enough to wait for others.

To wait for many others.

Sarah looked at the laptop. She brought up the Creature Feature game. Its small images began to dance on the screen. Maybe these are special images, she thought. Rats like only these images . . .

The game's background music began to play. The waltz music. She had turned the volume down, and could hardly hear it.

LA DA DA DUM . . .

LA DEE DA DA, DA DUM . . .

She recalled Surfer.

Spinning.

He'd spin around like a dancing mouse.

"IT'S THE MUSIC," she suddenly screamed. "IT'S GOT TO BE THE MUSIC."

Michael jumped at her shout. He saw her pressing the volume control on the laptop keyboard. The music became louder, stronger. She put the microphone right on the computer speaker, and turned the PA up to its full amplitude. The music from the computer game blasted out of every speaker on the pier.

LA DEE DA DA, DA DUM . . .

DA, DA DUM . . .

Sarah saw something was happening—as though the black wave of death was cresting, its motion on the glowing screens slowing like waves that had rolled as far as possible onto a shore. The rats began to stop chewing their way into the control room. The few rats that were already on the floor wandered docilely toward the crack of a doorway. Sarah and Michael rushed to the glass windows and stared down. The horde of rats had stopped their onslaught and had turned to stare at the speakers.

Angry, terrified people began to understand the attack was over. Sarah sighed audibly. She put her arm around Michael, and the two of them sat exhausted on a hard stainless-steel bench.

Over. All over.

The words drifted through Sarah's mind like a mantra. A prayer. For a moment she closed her eyes and thought about sleep. Rats fading. The music is working. Everything will be fine—

But . . .

CRASH.

The wall behind them shattered. A massive,

burned and scarred thing with glaring yellow eyes and a mouth of dagger teeth burst into the control room. Sarah and Michael were on their feet screaming. Sarah recognized the mutilated pebbled snout, a head with only holes left for ears and blackened legs ending in sickle claws.

It can't be, Sarah shrieked in her mind.

The emperor. The fire. Fire. The king survived. Survived the fire. A sluice . . . there must have been a sluice with a rapid flow of water and . . .

A swim of hate and revenge . . .

Sarah threw Michael ahead of her so he'd be behind the center console. Trembling—gasping . . . she raced to follow him but the mutant had moved with astonishing speed and was already in the air. Its hugeness struck Sarah in the back, its hot stinking breath and vomit dripped on her neck.

Oh, God, no.

Sarah's knees were buckling, sweat pouring from beneath her arms as the ground rushed up to smash her face.

"Save yourself!" Sarah shouted at Michael.

She saw Michael struggling to open the door, as the giant rat clawed at her, turning her to him. His ripped and burned body was over her now, provoked and shaking like an attacking crocodile.

CHIRRRRR. CHIRRR.

The emperor was trying to bite her face, but she kicked at him, slashed at his grisly snout and laser eyes. Her heart convulsed in her chest as a claw struck the side of her head. There was a sharp pain in her temple, but somehow she kicked again and was out from under him. The room tilted crazily as she struggled to her feet. Her eyes searched the glowing dials of the console. She saw her laptop.

Her laptop with its electrical cord. She had a moment while the mutant rat licked at itself before it turned toward her. In that moment, Sarah became totally aware, as if her mind were able to drink in all the possibilities of the room at once. She saw Michael pressed against the wall next to the water cooler. She knew their only chance, the only thing they could do.

She grasped the laptop. For a moment she remembered Michael had frozen in the kitchen. She remembered yelling at him. "Hit the switch!" Sarah had cried when a rat was trapped in the disposal. "Hit it!" But he had frozen.

But now she didn't have to say words.

He pushed suddenly, violently, against the water cooler and its glass jar tilted. The entire base jack-knifed out from under it, and the water bottle hurtled down to the tile floor. The glass shattered and a wave of water rushed toward the giant attacking rat. It was coming fast into the cascade, its feet sweeping through the instant pool. Sarah threw the laptop down.

The computer with its glowing screen and its music and its electrical cord. It exploded on the wet tiles, its screen and plastic shattering into a frenzy of sparks and electric crackling. The voltage climbed like a shimmering blanket to surround the body of the emperor rat, and his body shook as the electricity riddled him.

The giant rat fought to resist, to struggle out of the crackling field but the convulsions were stronger. Consuming. A moment longer and his heart burst and he crashed dead into the wetness. There was the smell of melting flesh and electrical wires and finally the terrible crackling stopped.

. . . now there were other sounds.

Sarah managed to open the locked door of the control booth—and she saw her father. She and Michael ran to him and he put his arms around them.

There was uproar on the pier. The mob had turned, shouting at the becalmed rats, and the people began to slaughter them.

Music soothed the savage beasts . . . soothed them . . .

The crowd cried out, stomping wildly, clubbing rats, using bats and golf clubs and anything they could get their hands on. The monitors showed military men in shining suits—like space suits!—arriving. Rushing on to the pier along with more soldiers firing guns. The men in shining suits had tanks on their backs and held funnels that dusted the rats by the hundreds.

Thousands.

Whole blankets and tarpaulins of rats.

Military exterminators rushing among the rodents and killing them. Toward the end, the few rats that weren't killed leaped from the pier. They rained down into the river and appeared to dive under the water, pulling human corpses with them toward the labyrinth of sewer pipes and tunnels beneath the city.

Mack Macafee held both his kids even tighter.

"Thank God, you're all right," he said. "Thank God."

He looked at Sarah, and when he could finally believe it was all over, he said, "I'm very proud of you. What you did . . . you saved thousands of people. You saved us . . ."

Sarah brushed away the hair from her face and

looked at her father. For the first time since their mother's death, Sarah saw something in her father's eyes that she had long waited and hoped to see. The way he looked at her made her understand completely that the danger was really over. All of it.

The lurking dangers.

The buried dangers.

And she knew the silences between them would go away. No more silences in the family—between her or Michael—or any of them. They wouldn't pretend anymore about anything. It would be very different than it had been. They'd speak up when there was trouble . . . when trouble might come again.

They'd talk.

Let light into the corners.

There would be no smoldering secrets, nothing hiding in dark places. On this night—in this moment—they knew in spades, that covering-up can come back to haunt.

Acknowledgments

I wish to thank my sister, Mrs. John Hagen, for our many visits and rodent discussions in New Jersey diners. I want to thank my friends Vincent and Ed and Richard and Hiroshi and Spencer and his lovely Maura—all those who had to put up with my crazed calls as the rats tried to devour me. Much appreciation to the many librarians and teachers who shared their ideas and students and imaginations and courage with me: Gracelyn Fina Shea; Barbara Younkin; Joyce Cope; Thelma Gay; Florence Butler; Jean Lukesh in Nebraska; Jennifer Goebel; the remarkable Teri Lesesne; Jami Hradecky and all my Dallas friends; Anne Hage; Karen Lloyd and her husband—and wonderful son and daughter, who let their pet rats crawl all over me.

Thank you to the many other teachers and librarians in schools who have fabulously affectionate pet rats with which to play. My annual gratitude goes to my other Michigan pals and brain engineers, Cindy and Lynn and Deborah and Sue—and their fab and brill families. Finally, my thanks to my son, David, and daughter, Lizabeth, who are always there for me when things go bump in the night.

And to all who want to e-mail me, my address is PaulZindel@AOL.com